No Time Like the Present

Timber Falls, Volume 6

Fiona West

Published by Tempest and Kite, 2021.

This is a work of fiction. Similarities to real people, places, or events are entirely coincidental.

NO TIME LIKE THE PRESENT

First edition. September 24, 2021.

Copyright © 2021 Fiona West.

ISBN: 978-1-952172-29-8

Written by Fiona West.

CHAPTER ONE

TWO YEARS AGO

The further they got away from the airport, the more Tharushi Udawatte knew she had made a gigantic mistake. The smiling white man with dark hair sprinkled with gray who'd picked her up was still smiling at her as she sat in the passenger seat. The only thing keeping her from freaking out was the quiet classical music playing from the car's speakers.

"Is this your first time in Oregon?"

She nodded, regretting sitting up front. It hadn't been a long flight from Chicago, but traveling always took it out of her. Maybe if she'd sat in the back, he would've left her alone. Then again, this guy—Dr. Durand—seemed pretty determined to be friendly.

"Oh, you're going to love it here. You can't beat Oregon for fresh fruit and fresh air."

Based on her preliminary research, they grew a lot of grapes here for wine, but as she looked out the window, she mostly saw cows, horses, and sheep grazing, perhaps the odd alpaca. When she'd looked at it on the map, she hadn't realized it was so...rural. The drive from Portland was only a little over an hour; in Chicago, an hour in a car wouldn't even get her outside the city.

Not that she did that often; taking Metra or the El was more convenient.

"My second son, Kyle, will be helping with the interns, and my youngest son's in your program." He glanced at her. "I know you don't know many people here, but Daniel's a pretty friendly guy. He's a good kid. Hopefully you can help each other out."

"Hopefully," she agreed, not particularly meaning it. If the son was anything like the father, she was probably going to be too annoyed to make friends with him. She preferred to keep to herself. But she should give him a chance; her mother had scolded her just before she left about not writing people off too quickly. Tharushi didn't agree. Snap judgments weren't wrong if they were accurate; she could read some people the minute she met them, and if she knew they weren't going to get along, what was the point in putting effort into a relationship of any kind? In general, she didn't click with extroverts like Dr. Durand. It would be good to have colleagues she could depend on, but beyond that, she was here to work and to learn. Period.

"Where are you staying?" Dr. Durand asked as he merged onto an exit ramp off I-5.

Oops; yes, that was probably helpful information for the person dropping her off to have. Since the program at Santiam Hospital had arranged her housing and airport pickup, she assumed he'd been given that information. Tharushi pulled her travel paperwork folder out of the thin pocket in the middle of her backpack. "It's at 45 Coho Lane, Apartment One."

"Oh, Apartment One, huh?" He chuckled, and she wasn't sure what was funny. "Is that Dennis and Mildred Wilson's apartment?"

"Yes, they are my landlords. Do you know them?"

He smiled again. "Yeah, you could say that. I've been their doctor for about thirty years. Seen them through broken bones, asthma attacks, chickenpox, all that stuff. He was our Spanish teacher at the high school until he retired a few years ago. I'm not sure how he's spending his time now, besides the odd golf game."

Good, she thought, *then hopefully the apartments will be kept in good shape.*

"I'll be sharing the apartment with another resident."

"Makes good sense, given the housing shortage around town. Do you know who it is?"

"Dr. Trout, I believe."

"I haven't met him yet, but I think he's from northern Washington, right up along the Canadian border. He went to Washington State for his undergrad and UW for medical school, so he seems to be happy being close to home." He said it like "you-dub," and for a minute she didn't know what he was talking about. Where she was from, UW meant University of Wisconsin, not University of Washington.

If you haven't met him, how do you know so much about him? If he was going to gossip about her, she wasn't interested in telling him anything. She would reveal herself to her colleagues in her own time and in her own way. If it contributed to being called stuck up or conceited, so be it. Her mother's parting advice, whispered in her ear at the airport as her brothers and her father argued about who was going to carry all her luggage, came back to her...*try to stay soft.* She knew what she meant; new situations made her tense.

"Okay, okay, Amma, quit hogging her," her brother Ravi had said, pulling her into a hug with one arm around her neck, squeezing her through her mass of curls. He still hadn't shaved the ridiculous mustache he'd grown over the summer while he was clerking for Judge Boyd, and it tickled against her forehead. "Be good, nangi. Don't walk alone at night."

"It's not a city," she'd said, pushing him off. "And I'm twenty-eight years old."

"It doesn't matter how old you are, problems can come at any time," her father had said in his commanding baritone. "You know that Praati, your auntie Selma's daughter? She was living in a small town and got run over by a car." That wasn't true; she'd just been splashed once by a big truck going by.

"I'm going to get a car," she'd promised again. "Seriously. Just relax."

Dr. Durand turned off the interstate, and the landscape changed...Walmart and Wendy's gave way to barns and grass. They passed a sign for Silver Falls State Park.

"Is Timber Falls near Silver Falls?"

"No, not really. Silver Falls is farther south, and it's more of a tourist destination. Timber Falls mostly attracts locals looking for a place to picnic. Now Multnomah Falls, that's the one that draws international attention..." The man continued to rate the waterfalls of his home state while Tharushi looked out the window, nodding and smiling when it was appropriate. After a while, he must have noticed her interest in the music, the way her fingers drummed against her knee in time.

"You like Beethoven?"

Like? No, like wasn't a strong enough word. Music kept her alive. She loved medicine, but medicine was her occupation, not her vocation.

"Yes." She could inform him that she'd been playing piano since she was big enough to pull herself up onto the bench, that she still had the toy piano her dad had bought for her fourth birthday. That she'd started lessons at age six, that it was how they bribed her to pay attention in school, which seemed pointless to her. But she left it at *yes.*

Dr. Durand went back to pointing out things about the landscape as the trees crowded the road on either side, creating a tunnel that felt to Tharushi like it was closing in. Somehow, walking the Magnificent Mile in downtown Chicago felt less claustrophobic. Finally, he turned off the narrow highway onto a gravel road. It was still a quarter of a mile before they'd reach their destination, according to her phone's map app. They bumped and rocked their way down the road until he cheerfully announced, "Here we are!"

She peered through the windshield. The white farmhouse looked like it had been built in the early 1900s; it was too square for more modern architecture. It was surrounded by what looked like an impressive garden in warmer months: the roses lacked blooms, and the irises drooped a bit. They seemed to have tucked daisies and clumps of lilies and azaleas anywhere there was room. The foliage of what appeared to be large lilac trees brushed up against the house as a bracing wind gusted suddenly between the buildings. A freestanding garage, also white, stood about thirty feet away. Leading up the side was a pair of wooden steps with a railing that looked improvised.

"Where's the apartment?" she asked, still confused.

"It's over the garage," Dr. Durand said, pointing toward the deathtrap stairs just as drops of rain began to pepper the windshield.

She should've asked more questions. She should've asked for pictures. Having been rejected by other programs, she'd snatched up this one as a chance at redemption. It turned out redemption looked like a weird attic in the middle of the woods, probably infested with spiders. She absolutely would not be able to drag her suitcases into it without assistance. This was not an apartment. Apartments were squat brick buildings with a bunch of doors and neighbors who ignored each other unless they got the wrong mail. This was...something else.

The door at the top of the stairs opened, and a man with floppy blond hair came out. The rain left dark spots on his white T-shirt as he jogged down to the car.

"You must be Dr. Durand," he greeted her chauffeur, and the two shook hands, exchanging mild pleasantries, as she exited the car. "And you must be my new roommate. I'm Greg Trout." He shook her hand, too, and his grip was firm. "Isn't this place something else?"

"I was just thinking that," she replied honestly.

"Smell that pine air. So fresh! So great. Love it." He took a deep breath and let it out, his breath fogging in front of him. "Can I help you with your suitcases?"

"No, I've got it," she said quickly.

In fact, Dr. Durand had beat them to it and was already hauling both of them upstairs.

Dr. Trout gestured for her to lead the way. Tharushi grabbed her backpack and started up. Greg was still talking.

"The landlord, Dennis, said he's going to add some tread to these steps so they're not so slippery when they're wet. It's a pretty damp area here, as I understand it, so watch your step. Nice guy, Dennis. He did have kind of a long list of projects he mentioned, so if there's something you need sooner rather than later, I'd let him know. He said he'd be over to meet you when they get back from dinner with their grandkids. Apparently, it's a Saturday tradition."

"Okay." She realized she'd never shouldered the backpack; she was just carrying it in front of her like a security blanket. It sort of was; anything that housed her passport, birth certificate and wallet had to be considered something to be guarded closely. "Which room is mine?"

"I gave you the one connected to the bathroom." He pointed at the other end of the open space. "Mine's over there. That okay?"

"Sure," she said, just wanting to go into her room and close the door and be done for today. Unexpectedly, tears sprang to her eyes. *I'm just tired. This is fine.* And in truth, it would probably look fine tomorrow. From the front door, there was a TV on the wall to her left and a large black futon in the middle of the room with a cream rug under it. Behind it, against windows that looked out on the woods, sat a small kitchen table. The galley-style kitchen was also crammed into a small space to her left. Her door was next to that, and she assumed the other door on the far wall was the bathroom he'd mentioned. There was no piano; it had been a foolish hope, but she didn't realize how deeply she'd been holding onto it until it was ripped from her hands by reality.

"You good?" Dr. Durand asked, eyeing her a bit warily.

"Yes." She would be. She would make this work and salvage her career.

"All right. Here's my number." He handed both of them a business card. "Let me know if you two need anything."

"Will do. Thank you, sir." Greg shook his hand again, and Dr. Durand gave her a wave as he left, smiling. *Always smiling.* She was still standing by the front door, trying to breathe, that strange tree scent he'd mentioned somehow stronger in the house. Maybe it was the wood floors.

"You want the ten-cent tour?" Greg asked. "I mean, I've only been here half a day, but I figure it's better than nothing."

"No, I'll...just give me a minute."

"Sure."

She lurched across the open space to the bathroom, still clutching her backpack, figuring that was a reasonable place to start collecting herself emotionally. And worst-case scenario, to throw up.

CHAPTER TWO

GREG TROUT WAS IN HEAVEN. He'd woken up early, too excited to sleep, and slipped out of the apartment to explore the beautiful area around the apartment. The ground under his feet was frozen and he left melty footprints as he ventured toward the woods. His hands were tucked tight into his fleece-lined pockets, and he was thankful for his hat. The air here was so wet; on the farm, he'd rarely worn a stocking hat, even though it was colder than this. It had been wet in Seattle, too, but not this cold.

He stopped to look at a spider web, lace-edged with frost. There was a little deer path into the woods, and he followed it, ducking under the odd branch that tried to bar his way. It led uphill, and the farther up he climbed, the more he wondered where it was going. He didn't want to go too far from the apartment. It wouldn't do to be known as the intern who got lost in the woods before his residency even started. *I'm already older than most of the others, I'm sure.*

The phone in his pocket buzzed, and he pulled it out to read the text.

Dad: Good morning! How was your first night in the new digs?

Greg: Morning! Not bad.

Dad: How's the roommate?

Greg: Seems nice enough.

She hadn't exactly seemed comfortable last night, though. As far as he knew, she hadn't touched the lasagna he'd made, and she didn't have a car unless she called Dr. Durand. He wanted to let her know he could run her to the store; he'd driven down his truck. Maybe she was gluten-free. Maybe she was dairy-free. Maybe she was both. At any rate, she'd need to eat at some point, and he could facilitate that. Maybe he could take her car shopping, too. He had nothing else to do before they started work on Monday. He was just about to put the phone away when it buzzed again, and Greg sighed.

Dad: Well, we're sure proud of you. You worked hard to get here.

Greg: Thanks, Dad.

Dad: Bluewater will be lucky to have a doctor like you.

Greg sent a smiling emoji back and found himself grinning as he tucked the phone back into his pocket. Moments free of cares or responsibilities had been fleeting the last few years, so he just stood at the top of the hill and breathed. The path threaded back down the other side of the hill between the trees. A chipmunk with a black stripe down its back scurried out of a hole, stared at him, then scurried back in. *Woodland creatures. Magical.* They had small creatures on the farm in Bluewater, Washington, a very ironically dry place, but they were mostly gophers and rats that tried to eat their crops. He'd never stopped to admire how cute they were, because they weren't. Also, it felt at odds with being responsible for getting rid of them.

Now that his breathing had slowed, he heard water running nearby. Curiosity drew him farther down the hill toward the sound, and when the trees thinned, a lake lay at the bottom. Not a ripple on its surface, it sat nestled by hills, mimicking the gray sky. He sat down on a huge rock. An osprey swooped low, snatching a fish out of the water, disrupting the calm and sending ripples outward. Greg watched it return to a giant nest, high on a platform on the west side of the lake. It was getting lighter now. He should head back.

When he arrived at the apartment, Tharushi was up and showered.

"Oh good, you're up."

She sat on the couch, texting someone on her phone.

"Do you want some breakfast? You're welcome to whatever I've got..."

She didn't look up. "I ate a protein bar."

"Oh, okay. Do you want me to take you shopping today?"

"I'll just call a car."

A...car? Like some kind of rideshare or something? "Wow, I'm amazed that's a thing here."

She did look up then, her brown eyes a little uncertain. "Isn't it a thing everywhere?"

"Not where I'm from." He helped himself to a bowl and found his box of rice cereal. "We had them in Seattle, though."

Her head was bent again, typing furiously into her phone. Then her shoulders sagged. "It is not a thing here."

"Sorry," he said, shoveling a huge bite into his mouth. "I'm happy to take you."

"I'm planning to buy a car," she said, as if she needed to assert the fact that she would be independent eventually.

"Good call. We're not really walkable to anything, as far as I can tell. Let me know if you want me to take you to a dealership or something. You can probably find a used one on the internet. I'll check it out for you."

"You're a doctor; what do you know about cars?" She folded her hands over her crossed knees, and he suddenly felt as if he were being interrogated by the high school principal.

"Well, I grew up on a farm, so we fixed a lot of our own machinery. I don't know everything, of course, but I can probably tell the difference between an engine that's running smoothly and one that's going to crap out on you imminently." He took another bite, leaning his hip on the counter. Geez, this woman was prickly. She stared at him coldly. He didn't know what he'd said that had offended her, but it was something.

"But I can just give you a ride, too. Just trying to be helpful." He tipped the rest of the bowl into his mouth, crunching loudly, then slurped up the milk. "My only plans for the day are to explore the town a little, drive around and see what it's like. Do you want me to let you know when I'm headed out?"

"Yes. Thank you." She flipped her phone over and over in her hands. "I think we should talk about apartment rules today as well."

"Makes sense."

"Keeping each other informed of our comings and goings. Announcing guests in advance. Things like that."

"Are you a social butterfly?"

"Not particularly. You?"

He cocked his head, thinking. He liked people, but he mostly liked them from a distance. He preferred his space to be his own unless there was a good reason. "Not particularly," he parroted, and she gave him a tiny smile. Well, at least that pleased her.

"Do you have any medical conditions I should be aware of? Food allergies?"

"No."

Tharushi looked up from her phone where she was taking notes, her gaze narrowed and suspicious. "I don't mean to be blunt..." That wasn't his impression at all. So far, it seemed like she either played her cards close to the chest or not at all. But then again, doctors tended to be medically nosy.

He smiled. "Please, go ahead."

"But I saw your EpiPen in the bathroom."

"Oh. Yeah. I have to keep one around, just in case. I have a rare allergy. It doesn't really affect me much, to be honest."

"What are you allergic to?" Her fingers appeared to be poised to take more notes.

"Sesame seeds."

"Oh." That seemed to pique her interest, based on the way she sat up straighter on the deep couch. "If you're eating a standard American diet, that should be pretty easy to avoid."

"Yeah. I just don't eat a lot of Asian food, obviously." He realized what he'd said a moment too late. "But you can! I just won't...partake."

Tharushi smirked. "Our diets are probably remarkably similar. Don't worry about it."

"Okay. Because it's really okay. I don't want to be a cultural jerk."

"As opposed to other kinds of jerkery?"

He smiled. "Sure. There are laundry jerks who don't empty the lint trap..."

"A sin."

"And dish jerks who don't rinse out their bowls and let the cereal get stuck."

"For sure."

"And phone jerks who keep everyone awake talking to their long-distance girlfriend."

Her eyebrows went high. "I feel like there's a story behind that one..."

He gave her a full grin. "I've had a lot of roommates. Mostly guys. Jerkery abounds, at times."

"Well, so far, I don't think that'll be the case for us."

He nodded slowly. "No, I think we'll be fine." He pointedly turned and rinsed out his bowl, putting it in the dishwasher. "So roommate meeting later? And maybe a drive?"

"Meeting for sure. Maybe a drive."

"All right, I'll let you know."

But when he knocked softly on her door later, there was no response. She didn't reappear until dinnertime when she came out of her room wearing leggings, a nylon coat, and a reflective vest.

"I'm headed out," she announced.

"Which way?" he asked, then paused. "Sorry, that was kind of invasive. I've got sisters, and my mom always makes them tell us which way they're headed."

She looked out the front door. "Uh, north, I guess?"

"Toward the highway?"

"Yes."

"Okay." He paused over his mac and cheese. "And we'll have that meeting when you get back?"

"Yes."

"Okay."

She stood there for a few seconds, letting the warm air out, then abruptly turned and shut the door. Her footsteps pounded down the stairs, and he sighed. This roommate and her one-word answers were going to take some getting used to.

CHAPTER THREE

EIGHT MONTHS LATER

"All right," Dr. Baker called over the chatter of the three residents. Tharushi nudged the men on either side of her and they settled down.

"Today, we'll be performing some basic surgical practice, thanks to Mr. Craig, our local butcher, who was kind enough to offer us some specimens to work on." Well, that piqued her curiosity. "If you can suture a pig's foot," Dr. Baker went on, distributing the trays, "you can suture a human being. And never forget, the person you're stitching up has to live with your work forever."

"He didn't send along any bacon?" Daniel Durand asked, and Greg and Tharushi chuckled. He did seem to be pretty voracious most of the time. Probably all that biking he did. Dr. Baker did not seem amused.

"Please take out your suture kits and get started."

Tharushi opened the plastic packet and pulled out the needle. As much as she disliked IV needles, these were somehow worse. As her attending had pointed out, her work would be permanent. She would be marking someone's skin forever. She glanced at Greg.

"You gonna get started?"

"I'm getting there..." He scratched his head. "Is the mattress stitch through the inside?"

"I don't know, my school used staples," Daniel said, rubbing his hands on his blue pants. "Who's got YouTube open?"

"Whatever stitch you want to use is fine," Dr. Baker said, walking to the classroom door, "but they should be even and tight. You don't want this coming loose. You have ten minutes; I'll be back to check on you in a few minutes." They all protested, Tharushi included. Putting a deadline on it made no sense; she'd take as much time as excellence required in real life.

"Doctors are busy people. We want to make you competent and efficient," Dr. Baker parried back as she left.

Competency seemed like a worthy goal...it was the efficiency that scared her. Doing things quickly might result in mistakes. And those were fine as a way to learn, but she didn't want to be making them with patients.

"Tharushi?" Greg said quietly.

"Mmm?"

"Why should you never rob a bank with a pig?"

"I don't know, why?"

"They always squeal," Greg quipped, and Daniel laughed. Tharushi just rolled her eyes and tried to concentrate on getting her stitches even.

Her phone rang. Actually *rang,* so it must be her mother.

She answered as she continued to jab the needle into the skin. "Hello, Amma."

"Are you busy, can you talk?"

"Yes, actually, it's 3:00 on a work day, so..."

"Here, I just wanted to call and tell you that your cousin Peeta is getting married in December, so you need to save the date. You know Peeta, he's a few years younger than you?"

"Yes, I know Peeta." *And yes, I know he's younger than me. Kind of tricky to get a medical degree and find the love of your life.* "What date is it?"

"We don't have the exact date yet."

"Amma, how am I supposed to save the date if you don't even have the date?"

She tsked. "Don't get upset with me, it's not *my* wedding. Also, you'll be home for Deepavali, won't you?"

"That's in November. I can't come home twice in the span of a month. And don't you want me home for Christmas?" It would be amazing if she got away for one of those events. All three was definitely out of the question. It was easier for Greg, who could just drive home. Even he didn't get away much.

"We never get to see you," Amma complained, and Tharushi held back a sigh.

"Amma, I'm trying to sew a pig foot together. Can we talk about this later?"

"You're doing what? I thought you were at work?"

"Yes, I am at work...I'll call you tonight, okay?"

"Not too late. Appaa and I were out late last night at the symphony. We're pooped."

Tharushi couldn't help but smile. Even when her mother used slang correctly (as she almost always did), it still sounded funny. "Don't forget the time change. And don't go running alone. And don't open the door to strange men. And–"

"Bye-bye, Amma."

"Okay, bye-bye."

She tucked the phone away and turned her attention back to her pig foot. The smell of the formaldehyde was starting to get to her.

"Your mom okay?" Greg's voice was low, and he leaned close enough that the scent of his cologne won out over the pig; it smelled like a forest, which only seemed right, given how much he liked the outdoors. Vetiver? Cypress? She didn't know.

"Oh. Yes. She's just..." She searched for the right word as she punched the needle back into the skin. "Amma." He was still watching her, and for some reason, she found herself going on. "She wants me to come home for my cousin's wedding. And for Diwali. And for Christmas."

"My mom wants me to come home for my birthday and Thanksgiving and Christmas, too." He shook his head. "She just doesn't understand what this program is like."

"I know, right? I've explained it thoroughly. She's not un-intelligent."

"My mom's married to a doctor and I live in the same town where I was born, so I don't have these problems," Daniel put in. "You should try it." He turned back to Dr. Baker and started asking a question about needle gauge. Tharushi stared down at the pig's foot. It looked like she'd tried the procedure blind-folded.

"Time. All right, show me what you've got." Tharushi looked over as both men offered theirs out to Dr. Baker. They both looked perfectly fine from where she sat, but their at-tending pointed out a few inconsistencies, and it had Tharushi sweating when she paused in front of her. She held out her very pathetic attempt, trying not to cringe. Next time she vowed to let Amma go to voicemail...but it wasn't her fault. Even if she'd had her full focus, she would've struggled with this.

"Dr. Trout and Dr. Durand, you're excused. We're doing rounds in twenty, so don't go far." The guys started to pack up their stuff, but Dr. Baker put a hand on her table, and Tharushi's heart seized a little. "Wait for a moment?"

She nodded. She watched with longing as Daniel and Greg both left...and to her surprise, Greg turned and gave her a confused look over his shoulder.

Dr. Baker put both hands on the table. "You need a little more practice. Let's set up a time to meet..."

She nodded, her cheeks heating. It was silly; everyone had weaknesses. This was one of hers. It wasn't a big deal. Dr. Baker kept talking, encouraging her to ask questions, letting her know that she was looking for someone to come and give them some extra instruction in this area. Tharushi just kept nodding until she stopped and she could leave. She blasted out of the classroom, relieved to be back to her regular work.

"Hey." Greg pushed off the wall and joined her quick-paced walk down the hall. "Everything okay?"

"Yes."

There was a long pause, but he kept stride with her. "Okay."

They walked in silence for a few more feet, but she couldn't take it. Since he seemed to be following her, she turned down a short hallway with an outside door at the end.

"She said I just needed more practice."

"I can help you at home if you want."

She blinked at him. "Um, yeah. That'd be great."

Greg grinned. "No problem. I'll smuggle us home some suture packs. And buy some bacon." She smiled, but inwardly she thought the word *home* would never apply to Timber Falls. Eight months hadn't changed that.

"Okay."

"Also, what do you give a sick pig?"

She blinked at him. "What?"

"Oinkment."

She shook her head. She was getting used to his sense of humor, but still. How could someone so young and single love dad jokes so much?

"What are you two whispering about?" They both turned. Martina, one of the nurses, stood in the main hallway with one hip cocked.

"Nothing." Greg grinned. "Why, did you hear something worth spreading?" He started back toward the main hallway. "Come on, we'd better not be late for rounds."

CHAPTER FOUR

PRESENT DAY, FIFTEEN Months Later

"Sweater?"

"Check."

"EpiPen?"

"Check."

"Tissues?"

Tharushi smirked. "They are entirely for you, but check."

"So's the EpiPen," Greg quipped, "but you didn't mention *those* so pointedly."

She smiled and motioned for him to continue with the list. It had become a tradition after attending so many events together...events in which Greg often forgot something vital.

"Gift?"

"Check. What did we get them?"

"Well," he said, straightening his tie in the rearview mirror, "their list was a little sparse actually, since they're merging two adult households, so we got them an electric tea kettle and a gift card."

"That is perfectly unsentimental," Tharushi said. "Well done."

Her roommate started the car and pulled through the turn-around near the main house to go down the long access road.

Once they got onto the pavement again, she would check her lipstick and touch it up. But right now, there was nothing to do but bump over the gravel road and talk to Greg.

"How long do you want to stay?" he asked.

She shrugged. "Up to you. I know you'll want to socialize."

"Are you going for a run after?"

She shrugged again. "I might. Let's see how late it goes." It was only 4:30 now, but they were serving dinner. "I can always run before work tomorrow."

"But you need your beauty sleep," he protested. If one of her brothers said that, they'd be teasing. But not Greg. "Seriously. It's going to be a heck of a week. You need rest." He turned on the radio. "Let's plan to leave right after dinner."

"What if there's dancing?"

One side of his mouth hitched up. "Hmm. That's a pickle. I do love dancing."

"Which is why I asked." It was safe to stare at him here, bouncing down this country road, in his lavender dress shirt and gray tie. She didn't like it as much as the butter-yellow one, which set off the natural blond highlights in his hair and made his pale skin glow. But seeing as it was December 18 and it was an evening wedding, purple was probably more appropriate. And maybe in purple, she wouldn't feel the need to watch him like she usually did.

"Do you know who else is coming?"

"Everybody, I think," he said, scratching at his leg. "You should've reminded me not to wear these wool pants. They're itchy."

She scrolled through her phone until she found the message she was looking for.

Tharushi: Don't wear those scratchy pants this weekend to Dr. Devereaux's wedding.

Greg: Check. Thanks for the reminder.

"Well, I don't remember that whatsoever," he grouched, and Tharushi allowed herself a small smile. *You never do.* But despite her amusement, she did wonder what had him off-kilter tonight. It was funny that mild grumbling and accusations counted as a bad mood from this man, but she'd learned a few things over the last two years.

She took a breath to ask him, but he beat her to it.

"This is our last wedding, you know."

"Yup."

"First Daniel and Winnie, then Kyle and Ainsley, now Sawyer and Starla."

"Three weddings isn't enough for you, Trout?"

She didn't see or hear Greg go quiet as much as she felt it. It was like a vibration that suddenly stopped; it was like when your washer finishes its cycle and you wonder why the apartment is so quiet.

"Guess not," he muttered. Two years. How had two years gone by already? It was like their colleague Daniel's wife Winnie often told the new mothers: the days are long, but the years are short. Tharushi felt that. She had one more year here before she started her cardiac-specific residency somewhere else. But Greg was done. He'd be going back to Hickville soon...not that this wasn't. But from what she'd heard, his hometown was even more rural than Timber Falls. There was a slow sinking feeling in her chest whenever he talked about leaving, like a penny dropped in a mall fountain. She wished things could be different. And man, she missed malls.

Greg parked near the back of the church parking lot.

"Why," she asked drily, "are we parking in another state?"

"Because," he replied firmly, "it'll make it easier to get out when we're done. No one's going to block us in."

Tharushi rolled her eyes, and he grinned as he tucked their present under one arm.

"Trust your chauffeur, milady." Greg offered his free arm, and she took it gratefully. Since she preferred running shoes to heels, she wasn't too proud to accept help over uneven ground.

The squat brick building looked much more cheerful than Tharushi usually found it when she ran by on her weekend fifteen-miler. Sparkly ribbon wrapped the columns by the front doors, and white candles sat on natural wooden pillars of all shapes and sizes. The dark, weathered wood made it feel more like a cabin than a church. The scent of forest from the pine and cedar boughs above the door wafted through the damp air, and out of the corner of her eye, she saw Greg grinning.

"What?" she asked, suspicious.

"Should've known the forest hermit would find a way to bring the woods to his wedding."

Tharushi smiled, too. Dr. Devereaux had been one of their supervisors at the hospital for a few months now.

"Sawyer's not much of a hermit anymore," a surly young man announced, thrusting a program in their direction. "Not with all of us around."

"Oh, I was just teasing," Greg said, offering his hand. "Dr. Trout. You must be Aiden." The boy nodded, then accepted his handshake, staring up a bit wide-eyed at him. Greg wasn't that tall really, but he was built like a bull: wide in the shoulders with arms like yule logs.

"It's great to finally meet you, Aiden. Thanks for the program." Tharushi knew what would happen next: it was the same thing that happened to her on a weekly basis. Greg would smile that warm, hospitable smile of his, and this kid would try to hold on to his bad mood...but ultimately fail. She'd seen it work on patients. She'd seen it work on their supervisors, nurses, colleagues, waiters, cashiers, anyone. Even her. It was profoundly annoying.

"Should we head inside?" she asked quietly, and Greg turned back to her.

"Yes. Good idea." Over his broad shoulder, he called, "See you around the hospital, Aiden! Come by any time, but especially if you're hurt!" Greg laughed at his own joke, and Tharushi shook her head.

"Ah, it's the renters in Apartment One," Evan Durand said, greeting Greg with a friendly pat on the back. "How goes it?" Tharushi hadn't seen him in several months, even though he stopped by to see Kyle and Daniel at the hospital sometimes; he seemed plenty busy with his own practice.

"Very well, sir. How are you?"

"I'm going to go find seats," she whispered. She'd learned: this kind of glad-handing could go on indefinitely with Greg. If she didn't save their seats, they wound up in the back where she couldn't see or hear properly. He gave her a nod, and she strode down the center aisle, trying not to disturb the delicate lace runner.

She sat just inside the aisle in the fourth row, leaving a space on the end for Greg and his long legs.

"May I join you two?" Tharushi turned to find her mentor and supervisor, Dr. Baker, standing at the other end of the row.

Tharushi noted with embarrassment that everyone seemed to now assume that she and Greg were together. *It's probably because I don't have a car.* She made a mental note to ask him to take her car shopping when they got back. *Before he leaves.*

"Of course," she said with a smile. "Are Winnie and Daniel not coming?"

"No, they are, but they're not accustomed to being on time, so I thought I could save them the rest of this row. No need for them to be relegated to the back."

She got it. This was why Dr. Baker was an amazing mentor. They were on the same page in so many ways. In fact, she'd completely supported her switch to cardiology as a specialty and made room for her in the intern cohort for next year. More than that, she knew what it was like to be a woman in a particularly male-dominated profession, and she didn't let it slow her down. She'd run this intern program, one of few rural programs of its kind, and although they'd made missteps along the way (like starting in January instead of June), she took it all in stride. And she balanced her personal life, too; she had an amazing boyfriend, daughter, and son-in-law, and her first grandchild was on the way. Tharushi had nothing but respect for the woman.

"Are you looking forward to a break?" Dr. Baker leaned closer. "Be honest."

"Honestly, yes. Very much."

"I'm sorry we couldn't give you time off last year, but medicine waits for no one. Not even Santa Claus, if such a person existed."

"Ooh, be careful," Tharushi deadpanned. "Your grandchild may not be ready to hear that."

The blond woman sniffed. "I can't imagine Winifred would put such silly ideas in the child's head."

"But her husband might." Daniel was a fun colleague, but she was glad not to be related to him.

"He is unusually dedicated to whimsy," Dr. Baker mused. "I'll have to ask them their preference."

Tharushi gasped. "You would lie to the child?"

"A small price to pay for staying in their lives and keeping them happy, however much it may chafe against my own sensibilities."

The music was starting, a peaceful piano piece that reminded Tharushi of a sunny Illinois winter morning...something about the smattering of high notes reminded her of a cardinal calling. She hadn't had a good flat run since she'd arrived here. There was no replacement for those lovely, flat paths the railroad had left behind.

"What did I miss?" Greg asked as he slipped into the seat she'd saved.

"Dr. Baker plans to lie to her grandchild about the existence of a certain holiday figure, and I miss running in the Midwest."

Greg's eyes widened for a moment before he chuckled. "To stay in their good graces?"

"In part."

"It's a harmless delusion, now that I think about it," Dr. Baker whispered. "I mean, really. Far less harmful than the tooth fairy. The presents will be supplied either way."

They smiled at their mentor, then Greg turned back to Tharushi.

"Because it's flatter?" he whispered, his eyes searching her face.

"In part."

"But you're happier here than you used to be, aren't you?" he pressed.

She thought for a moment. Those first few weeks in particular had been rough. *I couldn't have gotten through them without him.*

"I suppose so. But you also lack cardinals."

"Why are you lumping me in with the Timberites? Talk to the management, Peaches."

"If only I could," she replied primly.

"Peaches?" Dr. Baker whispered. Her gaze was quizzical, and Tharushi felt her face heat; she hadn't known she was still listening.

"It's a long story," Tharushi said before Greg could explain. This, as far as she was concerned, was also a harmless deception. Because it wasn't a long story, it just wasn't one she wanted told.

She'd been standing in their kitchen, hungry after her run. He'd left jars of all kinds of preserves lined neatly along the edge of the counter for days now, and she couldn't tell what the plan was.

"Are you going to eat these?"

He'd looked up from the couch where he was studying. "Uh, maybe. Probably. My mom sent a care package. You can have the peaches if you want."

She did want. She had relatives in Georgia and their summer visits had cemented peaches into her heart as the most superior fruit she'd ever tried.

She cracked the jar open and ate slice after slice, only stopping when the jar was empty. When she looked up, Greg's mouth was hanging open as he stared at her, his books forgotten.

"Wow, you really *like peaches."*

"Yeah," she'd admitted, embarrassed.

He'd found her indulging in them twice more, once in the middle of the night when she thought he'd gone to bed, and a nickname was born. But he'd never used it in front of anyone else from work. At the hospital, he was friendly and professional, but not overly familiar. At home, though...

Tharushi was distracted from the thought when Greg and Dr. Baker both stood up, and she realized they were playing Starla's wedding march. It wasn't the traditional one, but it sounded familiar...slightly sad, but regal, not terribly well-timed for marching. She glanced at Greg, who was grinning like he knew a secret. She tugged at his sleeve, but before she could ask, he whispered, "It's Princess Leia's theme from Star Wars."

Tharushi smiled. She knew Dr. Devereaux's fiancée had a strong interest in the franchise because he'd asked her opinion on a T-shirt that he wanted to get for her that said, "I know," with a large picture of Han Solo holding a phaser under it. She'd approved. She'd seen the movies a few times, more since moving here. But Greg's fandom was more in line with her interests; he watched *M*A*S*H* at least once a week.

Sawyer Devereaux came down the stairs to give Starla his arm; his black suit made him look suave, and he'd cut his normally longer hair. She wore an ivory dress, the hem of which fell to her knees. She turned and waved to her children, who sat in the front row with her ex-husband, Charlie. They waved back, the younger one frantic. Emily hopped off the pew and ran up to her mother before her father could stop her; Charlie was holding a tiny baby in his arms, making it difficult to lunge after her. The girl ran up to her mother, hugging her around her middle, where the dress was delicately beaded.

"Mama, you look MAGICAL," she announced loudly, and the congregation chuckled. According to the town gossip, Starla had been pregnant during her first wedding, so that was probably why they'd waited a bit to get married. Their normally easygoing mentor had been "ornery" lately, to use his word. Dr. Devereaux was more than ready for this wedding. Starla and Sawyer were grinning at the girl, and they both hugged her. Aiden, their surly usher, seemed exasperated when she sat back down; that had been her brothers, too, and it made Tharushi smile.

Since she'd now been to three weddings in this obscure little place, Tharushi could safely say that she had liked Kyle's the best. These two wore their hearts on their sleeves at all times, and that wasn't her style. And yet there was a warmth to this wedding that she hoped hers would someday emulate; she felt almost as if it was designed as an affront to the cold outside, as a refuge from the late-fall chill. The gold accents warmed the whole room and gave the sanctuary an ethereal feel, while the scent from the boughs made her feel like she'd stumbled into a woodland haven. It felt holy to her, a truly sacred space. Some uncle of Starla's was officiating, and in her opinion, the sermon was dragging on a bit long. The standard choice for Timber Falls weddings was a tall, dark-haired, tattooed man named Pastor Kellan, and she hadn't appreciated his brevity until now. But soon enough, it was time for the best part of any wedding:

the kiss. Tharushi did not pretend to be a romantic; in general, she thought most people's notions about how storybook life should be were pretty silly. But there was something special about a married couple's first kiss, and the Christmas feel in the air was only amplifying that. Watching her instructor take his wife's face in his shaking hands, it was clear that he cherished her. He cried, of course; she was quite used to that from him now, and based on Starla's grins and tender headshaking, she was, too. As the recessional faded, Greg leaned over to her.

"Well, wedding buddy, you ready to head to the reception?"

She nodded. She knew how it would go by now; he'd get her a drink, they'd dance at least once together, they'd eat dinner, and then go home. But knowing it was the last time had her stomach tightening and her appetite fading.

"And there's no reason to rush home. I'll run in the morning."

"Okay." He offered his arm, just as he had when he escorted her into the building, and she took it gratefully. She'd just be thankful for the time they had left, she told herself, however fleeting it might be.

CHAPTER FIVE

"GOT SOMETHING FOR YOU." Greg shook the plastic cup temptingly as he came into Anne Foster's room.

"It's not Christmas yet," she said, looking up from her book. Her friend Tansy Draper put down the phone she'd been using.

"This is a laxative, so it should help with some of your stomach troubles. Have you altered your diet lately?"

She shook her head. "I've been eating the same meals since Gary died."

He took out his notepad and sat down next to Tansy. "But you're eating regularly? Not skipping meals?"

She gave a slow shrug. "Sometimes I skip dinner when I'm not hungry. Just eat...um... popcorn or something."

"How's your energy level today?"

"Low. I didn't sleep well."

Greg frowned. "Was it because you're in a new environment? Did you have trouble staying asleep or falling asleep? Did you feel tired in the morning or is it mostly in the afternoon? Do–" Greg felt a hand on his arm.

Tansy gave him a knowing smile. "It's easier to answer if you just ask one question at a time."

"Right. Sorry. Forgive me for asking, but when did Gary die?"

"Two years ago."

Greg wrote that down. Her health troubles were probably unaffected by grief, then, unless this was some sort of anniversary. Even then, he didn't think that could cause this kind of abdominal pain, but these things were tricky. The mind and body were far more related than most people wanted to believe.

Abdominal pain was the bane of his existence. Most of the time, it went away on its own. But when it didn't...diagnosis was a pain in the belly for everyone. He hated that Mrs. Foster had been suffering for a while now, hence her hospital stay to try to nail this down. *And right at Christmastime, too. What a bummer.*

She cleared her throat. "To answer your questions, as I remember them, I haven't been sleeping well for months."

"Since two years ago?"

"No, only about four months, I guess."

"I remember you having troubles with sleep when we were in Paris," Tansy added, and Anne frowned.

"Maybe longer than six months, then."

"How much longer?" Greg tried to subtly direct his question to Tansy since her memory seemed to be a bit better.

"We went to Paris in May."

Greg wrote that down, too. It was likely that he would pass this case to Tharushi or Daniel, and he wanted them to have full information. The idea that he wouldn't get to see her discharged grated. Where he was from, you didn't just walk away from people in need. He felt his upset rising from his stomach.

"Dr. Trout." Greg turned at Dr. Baker's even voice. "I need to see you in my office at your convenience."

The upset bubbled harder. "Sure. I'll be right there." He closed his pocket notebook, even though he still hadn't had a chance to talk to her about her dizziness and trouble walking. He wanted to get her eating normally again first. "Let's see what that laxative does for you. I'll be back to check on you later."

"Bring more presents." Anne picked up her book again. Despite her joke, she still seemed subdued, and Greg wished he could offer her more hope, maybe even answers. But right now, they'd both have to be patient.

He was accosted by nurses who needed signatures and prescription permissions and had to detour for an underage patient who had wandered out of his room looking for his mom before Greg got to Dr. Baker's office.

He knocked on the doorframe, even though it was open.

"You wanted to see me, ma'am?" Tharushi was always telling him that it was *embarrassingly small-town* for him to call everyone ma'am, but he didn't care.

She smiled. That was weird. Dr. Baker was more of a stone-cold "get it right" boss lady than a friendly, parent-like boss lady. He didn't mind it (he had a great mom and didn't need another one), but the smile threw him off for a second. The only other times he'd seen her smile were when her hot dermatologist boyfriend Dr. Solokov stopped by to bring her lunch and when she was watching her daughter Winnie work.

"Please, come in. Shut the door." *Am I in trouble?* He quickly scanned back through his recent cases, but nothing came to mind. Maybe he'd worked too many hours? She was a stickler about them keeping to their time and no more. He sat down in the chair across from her desk.

"I'll cut right to the point: I'd like to offer you a job." In the stunned silence that followed her proclamation, she went on. "I know you've been planning to go back to Bluewater, but I'm hoping we can change your mind. You've been an excellent physician, and Dr. Grange is retiring from the family medicine clinic. Even if it was only for a year or two…" She let her gaze fall to the stack of paperwork on her desk. "We'd love to have you."

Dr. Grange had been dropping hints, so Greg had graciously told him he was planning to go home. That had always been the plan: get his degree. Complete his residency. Go home and fulfill his promise to Dr. Hernández. A year or two? Why would he stay for a year or two when he had a job waiting for him…She was looking at him expectantly, and although he was used to small-town style meddling, he hadn't expected it from his boss. It left him feeling a bit unmoored.

"Wow. Uh, thank you for the offer. I'll have to take some time to consider it."

She gave him a curt nod. "Of course. Here's what we're offering in terms of pay and benefits." She handed him a white paper, printed in a font he was now very familiar with: OpenDyslexic. *Which meant…*

"Daniel didn't want it?" His coworker's learning disability was no secret; Greg had been happy to study with him because it cemented the knowledge in his own mind, too.

"Since he's local, I offered it to him first, but it seems he'd prefer to take over his father's practice when he retires in a few years. He and his brother both."

Which meant she was also losing Kyle's help with the interns. She looked none too happy about it.

"I see. Well, I'm very flattered. Thank you for considering me. When do you need an answer?" He meant that; he didn't mind being asked second. Daniel was the logical choice to ask first.

"January would be fine."

"Great." They both stood, and he shook her hand. He opened the door and wandered back out into the hall...wow. He still couldn't get over it. It was exactly what he'd hoped for, the best Christmas present ever. Getting to stay with Tharushi would be...great. But at the same time, he didn't know if she wanted that. Didn't know what their future really held, if they even had a future together. He stood there as the traffic in the hallway streamed by him, wondering what in the world he was going to do.

CHAPTER SIX

THARUSHI HAD HER RULER out, measuring the thickness of the sugar cookie dough she'd just rolled out, her long dark curly hair draped over one shoulder. She frowned. Still not even.

"The more times you roll it, the tougher they'll be." Greg had been quiet tonight, and he turned *M*A*S*H* on as soon as they got home. It was unusual.

"It didn't say anything about that in the recipe," she retorted, and he smiled a little. "But it did say that they'll cook differently if they're not all the same thickness."

"Trust me," he said, focused on his tablet. He started the next episode he had cued up and set it on the counter where they could both see. At the familiar music, she smiled.

"Is this a Christmas episode?"

"One of the best," he replied, getting out the sprinkles. "Father Mulcahy gives the orphans a holiday to remember. And Winchester gets his toboggan hat and he cries."

"I thought you said it was a good one." She bent over to measure again, and he stepped back to give her space.

"It is a good one. He's just homesick. It's happy crying."

Tharushi hummed in acknowledgment and then rolled up her sleeves.

"I'll cut and you decorate?" she suggested.

"I'd say that fits our personalities nicely, yes."

"Are you saying I'm not artistic?" She tried to say it without a hint of annoyance; she just really liked to hear his thinking. The way his brain worked was fascinating.

He cocked his head. "No, just that you excel at the mechanical part of it: the cutting and the placement and all that."

She popped a bit of dough into her mouth, raising one eyebrow at him. "And you excel at sprinkling sugar willy-nilly?"

"Exactly," he said with a grin.

She snorted, and he leaned closer.

"Would you rather trade off?"

"No way," she said, bumping him away from the cookie sheet with her hip; he was just a little too close for her to relax. "You waste too much dough."

"I rest my case." Greg put his hands on the counter and leaned on it while she filled up the first pan, watching the show. It wasn't essential, of course, that the cookies were perfect, but she didn't like showing up for social events feeling like she didn't measure up. Hopefully, he would apply the same level of care he used in his work.

"You gonna take a picture in front of the Bean?" he asked as she slid the first tray over to him.

Tharushi let out a sharp laugh. "That's for tourists."

"Sometimes it's fun to play tourist in your own town."

She glanced at him, then back down at the tray, not sure if she wanted to tease him about this. Every conversation about their trips just reminded her how little time they had left.

"Is that what you do in Bluewater?"

Now it was his turn to laugh. "I'll make the rounds, but no, there's nothing like that to do. I could get a shake at Clumpy's. Jack's got peppermint this time of year."

Lord. How could he want to live in that one-horse town? She hated the idea of him going anywhere, but being so far away from where she hoped to be (i.e. an actual city) just depressed her even more.

"Why are you going back there?" Her voice was quiet, but her melancholy leaked through. A glance at his face told her the question surprised him.

"You know why. The town needs a doctor. That's why I went to medical school in the first place. Doctor Hernández isn't going to be able to keep going much longer."

"Right." He'd told her all about Doc Hernández the first weekend they'd met, and his absolute reverence for the man had not stopped since. There was no point in asking Greg to reconsider. She stared at his pan. "You made the snowman blue?"

"Of course," he said, like it was obvious. "What color am I supposed to use? Red? Green?"

"You could leave it plain." That's what she would've done. She knew she was too literal sometimes.

"Leave it–listen to yourself, Peaches. People need all the calories they can get this time of year. What kind of person would I be if I brought undecorated cookies to the party?"

"The practical kind." She smiled, then popped another piece of dough into her mouth.

"What–Oh, I see. You wanted this job for the scrap perks. Very unfair."

"You can have some, too," she said, pushing the cutting board toward him. But instead of grabbing a piece himself,

Greg just opened his mouth. Tharushi stared at him, wide-eyed, her heart thumping like the helicopter blades on *M*A*S*H*. *Was he serious? He wanted her to* feed *him*? A million excuses flooded her brain: it was too personal, her fingers had germs, touching his lips by accident might be unwanted...but she really wanted to try it anyway. *There's no point. You heard him. He's leaving.* Tharushi forced a smile and turned to the fridge to get out the dough for the peanut blossoms.

"Get it yourself, weirdo."

He grinned, then took a huge fingerful of dough directly from the bowl just as she turned back around. She slapped at his hand.

"That is not a scrap!"

"It is now," he said around his mouthful, devouring the delicious morsel. "Mmm. I put the sugar in the blender to make it super fine like my mom always does. So good."

"At this rate, there's going to be nothing left for the party."

"Don't worry, Peaches. I got you covered." He pulled the bag of chocolate kisses toward him and started unwrapping them. "Seriously, though. What are you looking forward to about home?" He was always asking things like that. She'd blown him off the first hundred times...she couldn't remember when she'd started answering honestly.

She thought for a minute as she rolled the balls in white sugar. "My mom's cooking."

"Yes," he crowed. "She only visited twice and *I* miss her cooking. What else?"

"Catching up with my brothers. They're not great communicators." Her last three emails to Pradeep had gone completely unanswered. Who didn't have time to at least reply *something*?

"Fair enough. What else?"

"Shopping on the Miracle Mile with my dad's credit card."

"Yes!"

Tharushi laughed at him. He was such a natural hype man. He should've been a cheerleader.

"Seeing the lights downtown. The snow. Seeing old friends. You know."

He carefully sprinkled some green and red stripes onto a candy cane-shaped sugar cookie.

"Yes, I do know. Substitute 'sisters' for 'brothers' and make them over-communicators, and that's my life, too."

"Oh?" She placed another ball on the pan and he squished it. "Backwater's got a Miracle Mile?"

"No, but we've got a spot for bonfires behind the water tower. Pretty sure it's just as fun and a lot cheaper."

She laughed again.

"And we do decorate our trucks for Santa's parade through the middle of town on Christmas Eve."

"I knew pickup trucks would somehow factor in this."

"It was a logical guess." The show was over, so he switched to Christmas music. She had the sneaking suspicion it was so that she'd keep talking.

"Are you taking a bunch of stuff with you?"

"What's that?" He'd been looking at the tablet still.

She kept rolling the perfect spheres, and he kept squishing them with the kisses. "I asked if you were taking a bunch of stuff with you. When you go home."

"Oh. Yeah, I guess so. Probably should."

She wished for the hundredth time that self-disclosure was easier. That she could hand him a book of all the shared moments of the last two years and let him read what he meant to her. Speaking of books, she still needed a present for him. They hadn't talked about it, but the previous year, he'd given her a day in Portland to just shop, driving her around and following her into store after store, waiting patiently while she tried things on. It had been the nicest present anyone had gotten her in forever. And it had given her a taste of what it might be like to date him...a taste she hadn't been able to get out of her mouth since then.

He fell into that odd silence again, and he was frowning at the cookies as if they'd insulted him, and that last kiss wasn't even close to centered.

"Hey, easy on the cookies there, turbo," she said lightly, and he seemed to snap out of whatever he was thinking so hard about. He scowled down at his work.

"I'll eat that one."

"Like I said. We're going to show up to Kyle and Ainsley's empty-handed, I just know it."

He smiled then, and she decided to get him something for Christmas that would make his smile last long after he was gone. She just needed to figure out what that might be.

CHAPTER SEVEN

AROUND ONE A.M., GREG was still staring at his laptop screen, sprawled on the couch in his pajamas. When they weren't working nights, Tharushi was the type who went to bed at ten no matter what, and she had long since closed her door. He stared at it. He rarely even knocked on it, preferring to wait until she felt like being social, but tonight, he wanted to march over and fling it open and tell her about the job offer. She was good at analyzing things; she'd helped him figure out countless medical mysteries. She had a gift for diagnostics; if she wasn't going into cardiology, she'd be a perfect fit somewhere like the Mayo Clinic. And then she could live in a city, too. She'd like that.

But some small voice inside told him that he needed to figure this out without her. If he accepted the job here, it had to be because it was what he wanted...if only he knew what that was. On the one hand, having more time with her might give him the courage to finally ask her out. It wasn't fair. If he hadn't chosen family medicine, he'd have another year with her here. Another year to gather up his courage and ask her what he'd been dying to ask her for eighteen months: "Tharushi, will you go on a date with me?" Instead, he'd be done with his residency in January, and they'd go their separate ways. He'd pick up where he left off in Bluewater, and she'd stay here in their apartment by herself to do another year in Timber Falls.

On the other hand, he'd be letting down the people back home he'd made promises to, people who meant a lot to him...but maybe not as much as her.

"Who am I kidding?" he muttered, turning back to the screen. "Even if I asked, she'd say no."

Her door opened, and his head snapped up. Tharushi was dressed in a lace-edged black camisole and shorts set, the likes of which he rarely saw her in, and he forced his gaze back to the screen.

"Hey," he said, trying hard to sound unaffected, even though he absolutely *was not.*

She shuffled to the sink and poured a glass of water, then downed the whole thing. Then she stumbled toward the couch and plopped down next to him.

"Can't sleep?"

She shook her head, and he noticed for the first time that she was wearing her glasses. She was basically blind without them, and he always marveled at how thick they were.

"Why are you still up?"

"Christmas shopping. I've got my mom and my sisters done, courtesy of Dr. Devereaux's mother-in-law's knitting and Mr. Powell's sheep, but I'm stuck on what to get my dad. He's so darn content."

"Isn't he in a wheelchair?" The comment bothered him a little, like a hangnail. It was just dangling there.

"Why would that affect his contentment?"

She rubbed one eye as she peered at the screen. "It wouldn't, I assume. I just meant you could get him stuff to go with it."

"Oh. I already got him a holy roller shirt last year." His dad had always been tough to buy for–actually, in a weird way, the wheelchair had helped, because Greg found all kinds of neat gadgets that he could attach to it to make life easier: a phone-holder, a water-bottle holder, a bag for his books. But Dad had mentioned that he was pretty holdered-out a few years ago, so now Greg was stuck.

"Have you tried asking him what he wants? My family just makes lists."

Greg sighed. "Yeah. He just said, 'I have your mother and my work. I'm good.'"

"Annoying."

"Right?" He sighed again. "Not their love, their love is adorable. But why can't he have a fandom? An expensive hob-by? Something I can contribute toward."

"Have you thought about a charitable donation in his name? He seems like a generous person."

"I'm saving that as a last resort."

"Get him a book. That's what I'd do. Something indie, not a bestseller. He can get those at the library."

He snapped his fingers. "Peaches, you're a genius. And I know just the one, too. It's allegorical. He'll love that."

She used his shoulder to help herself off the couch, and when she patted it a little, his heart bubbled like champagne.

"Happy to help."

He navigated to Bookshop.org to order through Books and Crannies here in town...but she wasn't leaving. He looked up.

In the dark, with his pupils still blown wide from the screen, he couldn't read the look on her face.

"You called me Peaches in front of Dr. Baker the other day."

Had he? He was usually so good about keeping her nickname between them.

"When?"

"At the wedding." Her arms were crossed now, drawing attention to her chest. He pretended he was searching his memory by staring past her into the kitchen.

"I don't remember doing it, but I'm sorry. I didn't mean to embarrass you."

"No, you didn't–" Now it was her turn to sigh, and she sounded so tired. "Never mind."

"I won't do it again. I'll be more careful. Here, sit down. Can I make you some chamomile? I–"

"No, Greg, stop." The way she said his name was just about the opposite of how he wanted her to say it. Right now, she just sounded frustrated. He sat, looking up at her, unsure how to make things better.

"I guess I just wanted to know...why." She shifted her hips from side to side, feet planted, arms still firmly across her middle.

"Why?" he echoed. "Why what?"

"Why you call me that in the first place." Her voice was low and had the same tone as when she went out to tell a patient's family things weren't looking good: vulnerable, yet a little bit sharp. Fear honed the edge.

"I don't know," he replied. *I guess I just couldn't figure you out when you first moved in. I guess I just slowly got to know you. I guess I just wanted to make a piece of you mine. I guess I just fell in love with you.* But he didn't have the guts to say all that. "I guess I just…like you." It was easier to say in the dark, and it was close enough to the truth to assuage his burning heart, set on fire with so much more than like.

Tharushi stilled, just staring at him.

"Do you not want me to call you Peaches?" he asked softly.

"No, it's fine," she said quickly. "I mean, it's goofy, but it's fine."

He mustered a smile. "I'm goofy too, so that works out."

She smiled too; hers was bigger and more genuine. "Yes, I'm aware. Are you gonna go to bed, goofy?"

"As soon as I finish buying this book. What about you?"

"I don't know. I'll probably try again in a while."

He looked down at the screen. "Your brain just too active?"

"Muscles are tight," she said, grabbing at her neck briefly.

Greg calculated quickly in his head. He'd admitted that he liked her, and she didn't run. She just stood there and smiled. And she didn't play it off completely as a joke like she had during their baking session.

"You want a massage?" he asked, and he was amazed at how casual he managed to sound. He kept his eyes firmly on the screen, terrified of what she'd say.

"Out here?" No, she wouldn't want him in her room; that was her fortress of solitude.

"Yeah," he said, closing his laptop, even though he was still on the payment screen. They weren't going to run out of books. "Just sit here between my feet. Or you can sit on the couch."

She gestured vaguely in front of him. "The coffee table's kind of…" Before she could get the complaint out of her mouth, he was up and trying to push it out of the way. When it wouldn't move against the rug, he picked up the whole thing and heaved it forward about two feet. Then he sat back down, knees spread wide, and held out his arms toward the newly cleared space. Tharushi crossed slowly, pulling her fingers through her curls. She crossed her ankles and sat down between his feet, and he tentatively moved her hair over her left shoulder. She tilted her head to the side as he started to knead the muscles between her shoulder and her neck. Outside, the wind gusted between their building and the main house with enough force to rattle the front door, and he almost missed her soft sigh.

"Feel good?"

She nodded, and he carefully avoided the flimsy strap holding up her shirt as he worked his way toward her neck, using both hands now. The light over the stove that they left on as a kind of nightlight flickered. Greg sent up a prayer that she wouldn't notice. She hadn't been a fan of storms since Day One. He ran his fingers down the column of her neck; she had such beautiful skin. Its bronze glow set against her black curls made his own skin look like a blown-out photo. He'd slid into a touch that was more caress than massage, and he made himself go back to working her muscles, switching to the other side. She was very tight, and she let out a little whimper when he dug his thumbs in too deep.

"Sorry," he whispered.

"S'okay," she whispered back.

"If you need some good neck stretches, there's a YouTube channel called..." He lost his words when she put her hand over his.

"Thanks, Greg." Yes, *that* was how he wanted her to say his name, like spiced cider, warm and comforting.

"You're welcome. Any time." She stood up quickly, wobbled a little, then righted herself.

"Sweet dreams."

"You too." He didn't get to see her face until she turned to close her door, and the flash of emotion he caught there was indecipherable in the nanosecond he had to observe it. There was a loud bang from behind him, and Greg jumped. He chuckled, remembering their first storm in the apartment.

"Greg?!" The knocking at his door was quiet but too frenetic for such a late hour. "Are you up?"

He pulled on his Bluewater Buccaneers sweatshirt in place of a shirt and hurried to the door.

"Tharushi?"

"Who else would it be?" she huffed, arms wrapped tight around her, covered by a purple paisley wrap. "Did you hear that noise?"

He frowned. "Just the noise of you knocking..."

"There!" she cried. "Did you hear that?"

Greg cocked his head to listen. There was a noise...the muted thump didn't seem like anything to wake him up over, but his new roommate seemed to be a bit skittish.

"The barn door?" He walked over to the windows that looked out on the woods. Sure enough, the barn door where the landlord kept his classic cars was open, flapping in the wind. "What did you think it was?"

She still seemed annoyed. "I didn't know what it was! It sounded like someone was coming up the steps." He could see that. Those stairs were kind of creaky.

"Would you go close it?"

He stared at his new roommate. "Now?"

"No, in the morning. Yes, now! Please?" This was like living with his sisters all over again. Granted, he thought as he toed into his boots, they would never get so upset over something so mundane, but they were not fans of going out into the cold, especially in the dark.

Greg grumbled his way down the stairs as the wind tousled his hair. He grumbled across the yard and around the back of the garage. He grumbled when the cold, wet chain didn't want to connect, the lock slipping from his fingers, too rusty and tight. Looking around, he found a stick and jammed it into the latch. He waited for a gust to rattle it, but it held. When he got back inside, not only did he not get a thank-you, but Tharushi was nowhere to be seen, and her door was shut. He went into his room and shed his wet clothes and hopped back into his warm bed, trying to get back to sleep as quick as he could.

The next morning, he found a note on the kitchen counter:

Thank you for your help last night. I went for a run, and I'll be back soon.

In truth, she'd come back with a gift card to Riverside Coffee, which she quietly set in front of him as he ate his cereal.

"What's this?"

She was already halfway to her room, but she turned back to face him. "Just a thank you."

He slid it away from him with one finger. "It's not necessary."

"You went out into the rain for me. I appreciate that."

"Then just say so. Neighbors help each other. I don't want your money." He knew he was being a little pigheaded, but it wasn't how he was raised. He didn't want to put them on a path where

this was expected every time he did something nice for her or vice versa. But her perplexed look said she hadn't expected his response.

"All right." She shut her door and he heard the shower run a few minutes later. She never did collect that gift card, and eventually, he tucked it into his wallet and bought himself a salted caramel latte. Every storm after that, he'd go out to check the barn door before bed. After the first few times, he found a steaming cup of chamomile tea waiting for him when he came back.

He'd been so caught up in his shopping, he hadn't gotten around to checking it tonight. "I don't need any tea," he called as he toed into his boots. "Good night, Peaches."

CHAPTER EIGHT

THARUSHI CUPPED HER travel mug of coffee through her mittens, holding it close to her lips. Greg was driving them to the Christmas tree lot. Hospital morale had been a little low, and Dr. Baker had asked if they'd go get a few trees to decorate for the hallways. If Tharushi had known it was going to be following one of the worst nights of sleep she'd ever had, she would've said no. It was too bumpy to drink, but maybe just the smell of caffeine would help.

"I could've done it on my own." Greg grinned at her. He clearly hadn't lain awake like she had; he was bright-eyed and cheerful as ever.

She couldn't get his words out of her head. She knew he liked her, knew they were friends, at any rate. He'd wormed his way past her defenses after a few months of living together. The outer ones, anyway. But there was a difference between fording the moat and getting into the inner keep. She knew she should've told him she liked him, too; she did. Of course she did. Everyone liked Greg. Well, except maybe Carter Carpenter. Greg had dated his wife Martina for a while last year before they'd gotten back together. Tharushi might be imagining it, but on the rare occasion that Carter brought his mother in for her appointments, she thought he glared at Greg a little bit.

It was Martina's father's Christmas tree farm they were pulling into, so Carter might be here. She took a large sip of coffee; it was bitter. She'd made it too strong in her insomnia-induced stupor.

"I said I would come. I'm here." *Besides, you think I'd give up a minute with you, knowing I'm about to lose you? Not happening.*

"And you look soooo happy about it," he teased as they got out.

"I'm happy," she muttered as they shuffled toward the table. They'd lucked out: Martina's sister Frankie was staffing the table today with Daniel's sister Maggie.

"Morning," she greeted with a yawn, and Tharushi lifted her coffee in salute. "Prices are here. We have Douglas firs in the front—those are the ones with needles all around the branch—and Grands in the back. Grands have flatter needles and branches. Questions?"

"Nope, I'm good," Greg said, squinting at the selection of handsaws like he was choosing best in show at the Westminster dog show. He picked one up, testing the weight in his hand and examining the teeth.

"You're cutting down a tree, not performing surgery with it," Tharushi deadpanned.

"Excuse me, it is *four* trees, and forgive me if I don't consider you an expert, Chicago."

"Yeah, you're the expert on killing things, Backwater." The coffee was starting to work.

Frankie was smirking at them as they started into the field, and she leaned over to whisper something to Maggie, who nodded.

"What kind do you think? Doug firs are traditional."

"I was going to say Grands are classy."

"Doug firs are smaller and easier to cut down. Can I assume I'm dragging these back to the truck myself?"

"No." She scowled. "I can help."

"Freshly cut trees often get sap on your hands."

Aw, really? She was already getting mud on the cuffs of her jeans. "I'm out."

He chuckled. "That's what I thought. So you are literally just here for the aesthetics."

"Aesthetics are important, too. If you get a Charlie Brown tree, how does that reflect on the hospital administration?"

He looked one up and down, then walked on. "It says that if they really care about how nice the trees are, they shouldn't have sent an intern."

"They didn't, they sent two. Now get cutting."

Greg looked at her like she'd just suggested they skip Christmas altogether.

"This, madam, is an art. Selecting a tree cannot be rushed. There's the overall shape, plus checking that it doesn't have wonky limbs or holes or..." He trailed off as he noticed her smirk. "Laugh if you want. But this is no parking lot tree situation. If we want good ones, we're gonna have to search."

She was so busy watching him, she'd stopped watching where she was going, and when she stepped on a slippery patch of grass, she started to go down. Greg lunged for her, and she managed to grab onto his wrist just in time to take him down with her. Somehow, he managed to let go of the saw, but he landed on her with a grunt.

"If this was a rom-com, you would've caught me," she groaned. He pushed himself off her with a mumbled apology, and she didn't think it was the cold turning his cheeks that shade of pink. Her coffee had flown somewhere, and the whole back side of her was now muddy. Greg was already back on his feet, and he reached down, offering her his hand. How was it that the dirt just made him look more ruggedly handsome, while she undoubtedly looked like a complete and total mess? She felt like a spa day gone horribly wrong.

"Aww, look at you," he said with dismay as he looked her over. "Let me take you home. I've got a towel in the truck..."

She put a hand on his arm. "I'm fine. Let's just do this."

He was scowling now, his gaze bouncing between her hand and her face. "But you took the brunt of the mud. I feel bad."

"Greg." She laughed. "Let's recap these events: One, I wasn't watching where I was going. Two, I slipped. Three, I fell. If you hadn't been here at all, the outcome would've been exactly the same. Well, except for my bruised ribs."

"Really?" The last time he'd looked that distressed was when he thought he'd burned the turkey on their first Thanksgiving together. *Not together. Just in the same apartment.* He put his hands on her sides, prodding them gently with his fingertips, and she decided to let him.

"No, not really. It was a joke." Mostly a joke—she did have a spot on her back where she was fairly sure she'd landed on a stump. But she was fine...more than fine, staring up into his brown eyes as he continued to probe her so carefully. "Did you hear me?"

"Yes," he murmured, letting his hands fall away, still frowning. "But I happen to know you're a dirty liar when it comes to your own well-being."

"It was just the flu."

"You should've let me take you to the hospital," he grumbled as he retrieved her coffee, trying in vain to wipe the mud from the rim. "It was sliding into pneumonia."

"It was not."

"Your lungs sounded atrocious. Your cough was like hearing a harbor seal bark." He was retrieving his saw now. "Just let me take you home."

"What about this one? It's suitably triangular."

He muttered something she couldn't hear under his breath as he circled it, looking at it from every angle, then sighed. "Yeah, it looks nice." He got on his knees, still muttering, and this time, she was pretty sure it was about the tree. She re-wiped her coffee lid with a clean corner of her mitten and took a sip. Still good. And so was watching Greg on all fours. *Don't leer. Don't make it weird.*

"Can you..." He sat up, brushing the pine needles from his hair. "Can you stabilize the trunk?"

"Sure. How do I do that?"

"Just reach your arm into the tree and kinda...hold it."

She squinted into the branches and found a skinny one to clamp onto. The scent of the needles being shaken off and the freshly cut wood filled her senses, and she closed her eyes for a minute. The fatigue was catching up again.

"Okay, stand back!" he called.

"Let go?" she asked, uncertain.

"Yup, let go!"

She did, and it fell away from her with a *whump*. Greg was already sweating, and now his knees were sodden and soiled.

"All right. One down. Three to go."

"Four. I want one for our house, too."

He stared at her. "We can't. It'll die while we're gone."

"I bet Mille would water it for us..."

"Peaches, we're leaving in three days!"

Tharushi shuffled closer to him, dipping her head to stare up at him through her lashes.

"No. Stop that. Unwatered trees are a fire hazard."

She turned her doe-eyed look up another notch.

"I know what you're doing," he said, wagging a finger at her. "Nope. Nuh-uh."

"Please?"

"We're going to be lucky to find four decent trees this late in the season. Five will take a miracle."

"So we'll take a reject. Put enough tinsel on it and no one will notice. It's our last Christmas. Please?" To her horror, her voice caught on the word Christmas, dropping to a whisper, and she felt hot tears threatening her like shoppers at a Black Friday sale. She looked down, but she could see his body language slump in resignation.

"Call Millie. They might be traveling."

Tharushi was already pulling out her phone. "She said they're not, everyone's coming here." *When did I start knowing or caring about my landlady's holiday plans?* This town had changed her. She wasn't sure if it was for the better or not; there was safety in simply nodding at your neighbors as you get your mail in the lobby. But that appeared to have been abandoned as a social convention in Timber Falls.

Tharushi: Would you be willing to water a Christmas tree for us over our break?

Mille: Of course, dear! It wouldn't be Christmas without it!

Smugly, Tharushi turned the phone so he could see, and Greg sighed.

"All right. But you're watering it."

"And we'll split the cost."

"I don't care about the cost," he muttered, but she saw his smile just before he turned his back.

This one, she decided, looking at the tree he'd already felled. They'd keep this one for themselves.

Now they just needed four more...

CHAPTER NINE

THE HOT SHOWER HE'D taken when they got back to the apartment had washed off the dirt but hadn't done much for his sore muscles. If Hector hadn't taken pity on him, he never would've gotten all five trees into his truck. Daniel and Kyle had offered to put them in their stands at Santiam, and Greg gratefully accepted their help. There was not much he wouldn't give for a bathtub and some Epsom salts right now. Unfortunately, he didn't think Dr. Baker would appreciate that during her holiday party.

Then, in the car, he'd made the mistake of bringing up car shopping with Tharushi. He'd offered to take her countless times over the first two months they'd been here, and somehow, it had just...never happened. He liked driving her, and she didn't seem to mind tagging along with him. But that wasn't going to work when he was gone...if he was gone. She was definitely upset about him leaving; that much was obvious. He'd thought she was going to start crying at the Christmas tree farm, and if she had, he didn't think he could've resisted taking her into his arms and telling her he could stay if she wanted him to.

"I'll deal with the car thing after Christmas; I don't have the bandwidth to think about it now," she'd said, her words clipped and cold. That was what usually happened when she felt overwhelmed with feelings—she just shut down. So her tearfulness at the farm had shocked him. Probably her, too.

"Did you tell her yet?" Daniel Durand appeared at his elbow, nursing a glass of eggnog.

"Who?"

His friend rolled his eyes dramatically. "Tharushi. About the job offer." Greg hustled his loudmouthed friend toward Dr. Baker's kitchen, which was thankfully empty.

"I don't know if I'm taking it yet, so no," he hissed. "And please keep it to yourself. This is complicated enough as it is."

Daniel nodded seriously. "Yeah, I get that. I mean, this is my hometown. I can't imagine being anywhere else. I told Sandra I didn't know if you'd take it."

Greg wiped a hand down his face, blowing out a long breath. "Yeah. I don't know yet."

Daniel picked up a peanut blossom and shoved the whole thing in his mouth. "You know what you should do? A pro/con list."

Greg felt his face squishing into a skeptical shape. "I don't know, man..."

"No, seriously. Here." He set down his drink and gestured in a "give it to me" kind of way. "Let's start. Pros of taking the job."

"I get to stay with my best friend. It pays reasonably well. I already know the system."

"Okay, cons."

"I break my promise to my hometown and my family. Dr. H has no replacement and can't retire. I betray the reason I became a doctor."

"Wow. Intense." Daniel put his hands on his hips. "When you put it that way..."

"Yeah. I know." Greg picked up a cookie shaped like a reindeer and inhaled it. If he couldn't feel his feelings, maybe he could eat them. He was going to gain ten pounds by New Year's unless he started exercising, and the sweater one of the women in his family was undoubtedly knitting for him was not going to fit. *Oh good, another thing to feel guilty about.*

"I don't even know if she feels that way about me. I told her I liked her, and she smiled and went to bed."

Daniel put a comforting hand on his shoulder. "Being married to a lady who is equally tight-lipped when it comes to feelings, I can relate. But I assure you, if she wants to give a relationship a try, it'd be worth it."

"You don't think it's too hard to be married to another medical professional?" Winnie was an excellent midwife, but it seemed like the two of them were always going in opposite directions. Though they had apparently found the time to get pregnant.

"Nah. Well, kinda. I mean, not *too hard*, but sometimes it is hard. But Tharushi's not a midwife; they work particularly weird hours. Cardiology should be more stable than that, schedule-wise."

"I keep telling myself that, but I don't know if I believe it." Greg paused. "Is Winnie here?"

"Yeah, somewhere...oh, shoot. I think I'm supposed to be serving punch or something. Hey, I gotta go." Daniel abandoned his glass and hustled back into the main living room. Greg followed rather than stand in someone else's kitchen by himself. He was drawn into a conversation about methemoglobinemia with Dr. Rose and Dr. Grange, and when he got more punch, Daniel was missing, so he served himself. Kyle was standing in a corner of the large foyer with his arms crossed.

"You okay, boss?" Greg asked, and Kyle shook his head.

"I'm overstimulated, and she's not feeling well. Ainsley's bringing the car around." He had Greg's sympathies. It would be difficult to be bothered by noise at a large function like this, as many autistic people would be.

"Oh. Well, that's good."

"Yes. It is." Greg stood with Kyle in silence, watching the rain fall through the front window. "Our party will be better than this one because we've invited far fewer people."

"Yeah, all of Santiam is a little much. Well, not all of Santiam, obviously. Night shift people always get the short end of the stick."

"Too much of Santiam," Kyle grumbled. "You're lucky you made the cut. See you then." He started down the stairs as Ainsley pulled up in her salmon-colored truck.

"Wait—how do you know I'm coming?"

Kyle gave him a skeptical look as he started down the stairs. "Tharushi already RSVP'd for both of you."

Of course she did. Pros: my roommate became my better half when I wasn't paying attention. Cons: she's not obligated to stay with me and come back to Bluewater. Though really, that wasn't what he wanted. She was going to be a great cardiologist. He would never want to take that from her. Almost no one knew how hard she'd worked to make that happen.

But he did. She'd spilled her guts one night, all about how she'd interviewed poorly for her residencies and didn't get placed, despite her good grades. Since he knew better now, he'd guess that her reserved, snarky manner didn't come off as caring and compassionate like doctors were supposed to, even though she absolutely was. Timber Falls had been a last-ditch effort to stay on track, but despite her initial discomfort here, she'd made it work. He wasn't the only one with dreams. He had to remember that. *Is this your dream, though?* He pushed the thought away. He'd made a promise. And he'd meant it when he made it. When someone saves your dad's life, you want to do something to repay them. This was what Dr. H needed.

But is it what you need?

Greg needed Tharushi. Coming home with her, even just as friends, was like climbing into a pillow fort at the end of the day. She was a good listener. Gave good advice. And he just loved looking at her, hearing her in the kitchen. Loved it when she came and sat next to him when he was watching *M*A*S*H*. But was that love? He didn't know. That was how his parents were together; he'd come home and find them snuggled together on the couch, just reading their separate books. Their love wasn't showy or passionate; he'd rarely seen them kiss. But he knew they loved each other...and due to an unfortunate vent situation in their old farmhouse, he also knew they were still making it work in bed, despite his dad's injury. He was glad, but he also didn't want to hear evidence of it when he was getting a glass of milk in the kitchen at 11:00 at night.

He needed more, though. This strange place between platonic friendship and being a couple was just hurting his heart. If he was going to stay, he wanted it to be as her boyfriend, not her roommate. Well, both would be fine. But not—

"You okay?" Tharushi was at his elbow, a crease between her eyebrows. Red was a good color on her. He should tell her that. He should flirt...say something.

"Yeah, why?"

"You're staring out the window moodily while there's a bunch of people in the other room to talk to. You're usually Mr. Social. Hiding during parties is *my* role in our relationship." The word *relationship* sent tingles through him.

"Just have a lot on my mind, I guess."

"You know this is not usually my favorite question, but do you want to talk about it?" She stood close to him, her voice low, and he wanted a hug so bad, it felt like physical pain.

"Not right now. Maybe later."

She watched him intently. "Your family's okay?"

"Yeah, no, it's nothing to do with them."

"Okay." She shifted her weight. "Do you want some food?"

"Not hungry."

Now she was frowning. "Are you not feeling well? Do you want to go home?"

"No, I'm happy here."

"You don't look happy," she pressed. "Why don't we just—"

"Tharushi, I'm fine. Really. Just—"

"There you two are!" Winnie seemed exasperated, and Greg shared the sentiment. "We've been looking everywhere for you. Should've known you'd be holed up together somewhere." Before Greg could protest that comment, she took them both by the elbow and started dragging them back toward the packed living room. "We're going to play Medical Pictionary, and I called you for my team." Greg went willingly.

Hopefully, the distraction would get Tharushi to stop asking questions.

Tharushi drew the short straw and had to go first. She drew a circle with a line through it.

"Contraindicated!" She pointed to him. Tharushi lunged for another card.

She drew a body, then put a dotted line through its wrist.

"Fracture!" She put down the card and got another one.

They got smallpox, benign, hypotension, malnutrition, and impressively, contusion. Winnie was beaming at them.

"I'm going to beat my mother for the first time," she whispered gleefully, rubbing her big belly. "Best. Party. Ever." As she predicted, they did indeed trounce Dr. Baker's team by fifteen points. The distraction was good, but Greg wanted to go home. Playing with Tharushi like this was just reminding him how good they were together, and that wasn't what he needed. His body hurt. His head hurt. He needed quiet and sleep and time to think.

The minute she got in the car, she turned to him. "All right, *now* will you—"

"I can't talk about this right now. I'm sorry, I just...I can't. I'm fine. Really. Everything's fine."

"All right." She was quiet the rest of the way home, except for the music she turned on. She was forever turning it on, but especially when she was upset, he heard it leaking under her bedroom door. *Music. That's what I should give her for Christmas.* But nothing so pedestrian as an album would do...he'd figure it out. It was a good idea. And maybe it would help say what he needed to ask.

CHAPTER TEN

"I'M GOING RUNNING," Tharushi announced as they headed up the steps. The party had been...difficult. When she wasn't with Greg, she'd wished she was, and when she was with him, she wished she knew what he was thinking. But in an unusual move, he was keeping his problems to himself.

She hated it.

"Okay," Greg said, but he still didn't sound happy. "You'll take your headlamp?"

"Yes."

"And wear the vest?"

"I always wear the vest."

"I know," he said, unlocking the front door, "but I promised your mom I'd ask."

Tharushi smiled. Her parents had initially had reservations about her sharing a living space with a man she'd never met...but after he'd photobombed her video call and insisted on meeting them, all was well. And Amma had loved meeting Greg in person when she'd visited a few months ago...she'd beamed when he offered to take them out to dinner in Salem. How he'd found that vegan restaurant, she didn't know, but she was impressed that he'd remembered her mom was a vegetarian and scored major brownie points. But Tharushi was fairly sure that in Amma's mind, she would somehow meet a nice Sri Lankan man who was slightly older, professionally successful, charming, and handsome, and they'd fall in love and get married. How this was supposed to happen was unclear to her. Amma wasn't biased: she seemed to like white Americans fine. And she hadn't minded when Tharushi had dated several men who weren't Sri Lankan during medical school, but...for a life partner? She knew he might not be Amma's first choice.

But it's not Amma's life. It's mine, she thought as she quickly changed her clothes. *And I'm the one who's got to live with my choice.* Of course, there was no choice to make. Greg *liked* her; he'd said so the other night. But it was as a friend. At least, he'd never said otherwise, and she certainly wasn't going to ask. A run would clear her head of all these pointless thoughts that circled but never landed. It didn't matter if Amma liked him if he didn't see her that way.

He wasn't there when she came back out to the living room to cross to the front door. She peeked toward his room; his door was open, but she couldn't see him through the gap. *Probably just finishing up that Christmas shopping. What do I care, anyway? He can do whatever he wants.*

A deer was eating Mr. Wilson's roses that looked up as she came down the stairs; she ignored it. Tharushi stayed on the main driveway that would take her to the highway, but cut over across the busy road to run along the river path on the other side. It was far nicer than running along the road, and the sound of running water usually had a calming effect on her soul. The river never froze all winter. It just kept bumping over rocks and tree limbs with its white peaks softly foaming, almost iridescent in the filtered moonlight through the cloud layer. *Greg would like this. He's probably out wandering in the woods again.* He'd suggested that she run there when they first arrived. Before she'd even stopped laughing, he'd just rolled his eyes and walked away. Paved paths were nice. And this would take her to the center of town, which was all decked out for Christmas. Wreaths hung on the streetlights; colored lights illuminated the little shops. Painted wooden cut-outs of elves were positioned near the street to point out the historic significance of the town's different holiday rituals...she would've never guessed they'd been lighting the Christmas tree on the same day in December for 89 years. The Baptist church had a huge nativity scene which she'd been informed would have live animals this year...good thing she wouldn't be there for that. Not with her flight leaving in two days. *Two days.* She hadn't been home in so long—too long, according to her dad. Truth be told, she agreed.

Tharushi let her feet take her past the center of town, which turned out to be a mistake as huge as the Christmas tree in the middle of town with its giant, spiraling silver ornaments. Because running through the middle of Timber Falls turned out to be not as introspective as she thought. She waved to Phil Durand, their physical therapist, who appeared to be taking his son Cooper for hot cocoa at Riverside. She waved to Deputy Painter, who was walking her big yellow dog. She waved to James Miller, one of the hospital's major donors, as he came out of the library. She waved to Farrah Durand as she walked an elderly client out to her car. She passed Carter and Martina Carpenter, but they didn't notice her; they appeared to be deep in a discussion about paint colors, bent over several samples, as they came out of the hardware store. Finally, the traffic thinned out, and Tharushi put on some speed up the hill toward the falls. The park was closed, but she just went around the barrier.

Her breath clouding in front of her, she stopped at the bottom and stared up at the wall of falling water. It was like medical work; it just kept coming and coming. There was no reprieve. But she was learning to live with the noise of that, the constant sense of unfinished work. Timberites were like that, too—she'd tried just ignoring their waves. But they just kept waving. Kept inviting her to things. Kept pulling her out of her comfort zone. *Two days, then I don't have to see them for three days.*

On her way back, she cut into the neighborhood just north of the center of town to avoid more waving. There was a back road she'd never been down, and Dr. Devereaux had told her it connected to the road their driveway was on. It would be nice to have another route...she had a little time. Greg wouldn't expect her back yet. Tharushi crossed at the light and couldn't avoid waving to Vince, one of the paramedics, who appeared to be on an ice cream date with Jennie Wallace. She couldn't fault the choice. She also loved ice cream, and peppermint was only available at certain times. One had to capitalize on the opportunity.

She took Bradford Avenue up and away from the highway; the terrain was steeper than at their house, and she lost her regular breathing, huffing and puffing as her legs burned. As it crested the hill, it faded into gravel, and she kept following it as it flattened out. The trees were taller here, unfettered by houses and asphalt, letting all the light take them to new heights. She was thankful for the headlamp...Greg was right, as usual. *I went running to forget about him, remember?* Her heart did not an-swer.

Tharushi started into the downhill, still *not thinking* about Greg and his violently handsome smile and his joviality and his quick wit and how good he was at outdoor things when her feet slipped out from under her, aided by the damp pine nee-dles along the edge of the road.

"Ouch," she complained softly. Her tailbone was definitely bruised. She tried to examine her scraped palms; not too many rocks in there. She picked a few out with a long fingernail, curs-ing her inattention and wishing the stinging would stop so she could get to her feet and go home.

"Mr. Oberst, this is the deal of a lifetime." Where was that voice coming from? Leaning forward, she peeked around the giant tree she'd landed next to, and saw three men gathered near the front door of a small blue house. The wind must have carried their words. An older man was standing in the open doorway, rubbing at the top of his balding head, fluffing his wispy gray hair. The other two men wore black suits, from what she could tell in the dark.

"This land's been in my family for three generations, but...I guess it's time now that Bonnie's gone. The kids don't want it."

"Your town's going to love having a VolumeMart. Trust me."

They will not. Tharushi didn't claim to be an expert on Timberites, but she knew this much: there was no way they were going to welcome a huge discount store like VolumeMart. It was one of those places where you could buy allergy medi-cine and shoes and potato chips and a fly-fishing pole all at the same store. At the few town meetings Greg had dragged her to ("What else are you going to do on a Friday night?" Um, anything. Anything else.), they were always talking about how to support local businesses. How to make sure people's dollars stayed in their community, how to use more locally sourced materials. This would shut them down completely. On the up side, she wouldn't have to go to Salem every time she was craving rice noodles.

"We'll send the paperwork over in the morning. But we're giving you an incredible deal. You'd be a fool to turn this down."

Tharushi got to her feet, partly in indignation and partly because the ground was really cold. They must have seen the flash of her headlamp because they all turned toward her. She gave them a wave, and Mr. Oberst waved back. The suits did not. *They're not from around here. What the heck is going on?* She could not abide it when people took advantage of old people. Her mother's father had been cheated out of a few hundred dollars by an internet scam, and she still got physically angry thinking about it.

"Who was that?" One of the suits asked, and Mr. Oberst answered, but she couldn't hear what he said.

It doesn't matter. It's none of my business. She would go home, take a shower, and go to bed. Put this weird day and its weird occurrences behind her. She pounded down the hill, watching her footing this time, and arrived home in less than ten minutes. Greg was sound asleep on the couch; he didn't move when she closed the front door. She removed his computer from its perilous position sliding off his lap and put it on the coffee table. But when she pulled the quilt off the back of the couch to cover him, he blinked awake.

"Hi."

She felt her lips curl into a smile against her will; just-woke-up Greg was one of her favorite iterations of the man. "Hi. You should go to bed."

He looked at his watch. "It's only eight-thirty." He yawned. The way he stretched and the groggy look still on his face told her he'd be back asleep in a few minutes, so she covered him with the quilt anyway. His mom had made it from T-shirts he'd had in middle school and high school, and it was cozy, but sort of uncoordinated, color-wise. Still, she'd never had the heart to ask him to keep it in his room. She'd already started toward her room when he caught her wrist.

"What happened?"

So maybe he was awake…because he was scowling at her minor injuries like he was going to write to Santa and have whoever had caused them removed from the nice list.

"I fell. I'm okay."

"Doesn't look okay. Here…" He got up and pulled her into the kitchen, never letting go of her wrist. "Just a little antibacterial action." Normally, she'd ignore his request and insist that she was fine. But it had been such a strange day, and he wanted to take care of her. The attention felt like she'd curled up like a cat in a warm puddle of sunlight on a winter's day, so she complied, watching his face. He seemed a little more like himself; maybe he'd worked out his problem. He washed his hands in the sink, patting them dry carefully, still frowning.

"Where'd you fall?"

"On a hill just north of the highway. It's a new way. Dr. Devereaux mentioned it; I think he lives kind of up that way." Maybe Dr. D would care about the VolumeMart, too. She paused; Greg was trustworthy, absolutely and completely, but she wasn't sure if she shouldn't just forget it. "Something kind of unusual happened. I overheard something I think might be a secret."

Greg looked around, as if someone might overhear, then playfully dropped his voice. "What kind of secret?"

"Mr. Oberst is selling his land to two men who want to build a VolumeMart."

His eyebrows snapped downward. "Now that doesn't sound like a Hattie-approved plan." Hattie Meyer-Bagsby was the town's unofficial mayor. She owned Timber Falls Paper Products, which employed a good chunk of the town's population, and one of her ancestors had started the town. So basically, she was Timber Falls' fairy godmother. Tharushi wasn't convinced she didn't have actual magic; she knew so much about the people in town and what was going on in every damp corner.

"I know, right?" She pursed her lips. "Do you think I should tell someone?"

He gently swiped the alcohol wipe over her skin, and she hissed.

"Sorry. I'm sorry."

Even though it still stung, Tharushi laughed. "Such a soft touch."

"Where I'm from, we call it being a gentleman." He scowled, his eyes still on his work. "Can I help it if I don't want to hurt you?"

"I can't imagine you wanting to hurt anyone."

His hands were warm and gentle, and even though she was starting to feel the sweat trapped in her running clothes in the warm apartment, she was in no hurry to move away from him. His gaze was sharp, trained on her scrapes, cleaning them with absolute precision. He knelt to work on her knees, rolling the fabric up carefully for better access.

"I did, once."

It took her a minute to remember what they'd been talking about. "You did?"

He stood and guided her over to one of the chairs around the breakfast table. "Yeah. I'm not proud of it, but...after my dad got hurt, I was pretty angry for a while."

"You had to put off med school, right?"

He nodded, his blond head bobbing. His fluffy hair was right there, and she wanted to put a hand on his bent head to comfort him. But she'd been keeping her hands to herself for two years, and this did not seem like the time to stop. And yet...

"I put off med school, and I was stuck in town, ferrying my sisters around and watching other people go off and have their own lives. And I was still on the farm, trying to keep things going, while my parents were drowning in medical bills." She had known that he'd had to delay, but not the rest of it. Tharushi's heart hurt to hear how he and his family had suffered. And yet, look at the man he'd become despite it.

Keep it medical, professional...

"That kind of injury is very involved."

Greg nodded again, but when he spoke, his voice was strained. "They thought maybe they could save his legs for a while. Those treatments added up real quick."

"I can imagine."

He stood up, signaling that he was done, and he held out his hand to help her from the chair. She took it, then quickly let go once she was on her feet.

"You made it, though," she said, limping across the living room toward her room. "You helped your family, and now you're going to help even more families in your community. That's...commendable."

Commendable? her brain snarked. *Really? Is he a general in some sort of war? Tell him how you feel! Tell him that he's an amazing, caring, open person, the kind you wish you could be. Tell him that you envy the trust that he carries around, even though the world's hurt him. Tell him!*

"Thanks, Peaches. I hope you're right." He sat back down on the couch, going back to his computer. And just like that, the conversation was over.

CHAPTER ELEVEN

GREG PADDED INTO THE living room the next morning, yawning. It seemed...brighter than usual? He went over to the window and blinked in surprise.

"It's snowing," he whispered, pressing his hand to the cold glass without thinking, watching the fat flakes drift down. "It's snowing!" he said louder, rushing over to her door. "Tharushi, wake up! Get up, you've gotta see this!"

He heard a sleepy groan and something thumped against the door. "Go. Away."

"No, seriously. Get up. Come on." She'd probably just thrown a running shoe, but he wasn't taking chances. His fingers hovered over the doorknob; he hated that thing. It wasn't just that it was cheap and brass and locked him out, but those were not points in its favor. He wondered if she was locking it. He kind of hoped she was, but didn't have enough confidence in his self-control to put his hand to it and see for sure. He knocked instead. "Peaches. Come on."

Through the thin door, he heard shuffling, dragging, and a moment later, the door opened. From behind square black-framed glasses, Tharushi squinted at him with one eye still closed.

"What?"

"It's snowing." He paced back over to the window, pointing insistently. "Look at it."

"I couldn't have looked at it an hour from now?" She wrapped her comforter a little higher around her shoulders but shuffled dutifully over to the window.

"It might be gone by then. It doesn't last around here," he explained. "Look. Isn't it beautiful?"

She leaned closer to the window to see out, brushing his shoulder. "Sure. Beautiful. Can I go back to bed now?"

"Okay. I'll be outside."

She was squinting at him again. "Doing what?"

"Making a snowman, duh."

"O-o-o-o-okay, weirdo."

"I'm the weirdo? You're missing the first good snow of the year! I think we know who's the weirdo here, and it's not me. Nuh-uh. No way."

Tharushi stared at him for a long moment, pursing her lips. "Be careful on the steps. I don't want to drive into work today." Then she turned and headed back to her room.

"Okay!" He'd just finished sculpting the bottom ball when she came down the steps, dressed in her shapeless heavy coat and black boots, holding a travel mug, her hair now pulled back into a tight ponytail.

"Where are you going?"

"Nowhere." She stopped next to him, her breath clouding in front of her.

"Did you come to help?" He didn't think so, but as usual, her dark gaze gave away nothing, so he couldn't guess.

"No. Just moral support." Tharushi took a sip of her drink, which must have been too hot, because she tsked a little at it, as if the liquid had hurt her on purpose.

"Moral support, huh?" He grinned. "And if someone should happen to lob a snowball at you, what would happen then?"

"That someone would regret it," she said firmly, and he smiled so hard, he thought his lips might crack. "Don't forget, Trout, I've lived where it snows. I am not a novice snowball maker."

"But your snow is dry...this is a whole different ballgame." He bent over and continued pushing the base of his snow physician around the yard, leaving a track of trodden green grass in its wake.

"It's not going to keep us from getting to the airport, is it?" She was staring up at the sky now, a solid sheet of gray above them, hanging dark and heavy. And the darker the clouds were, the more moisture they usually held.

"Oh, definitely not. I'll have the back loaded down, so we'll have plenty of traction. And I've got my chains. I'll get you there with enough time to hit a coffee stand on the way."

She was still staring at the flakes gently swooping down, and Greg found himself watching them light on her dark curls, sparkling. So he did what anyone would do: he scooped up a handful of snow and lobbed it at her. It clipped her shoulder and she startled.

"Oh, it is on, Bluewater."

"Hey, you got my town's name right!" He took a ball right in the face as payment for his distraction. It wasn't packed hard enough for it to really hurt, but it certainly did wake him up. He shook his head to clear the snow away, flinging it off.

"Bring it, Chicago." Greg ran and ducked behind the arborvitae and started stockpiling his ammunition. The gloves were slowing him down, but he knew better than to take them off. Any minute now, she'd...wait. He peeked between the branches. He couldn't hear her...there was no movement in the yard near their apartment. Where the heck was she? Greg stood up a little taller. She was clearly messing with him. Sure she was sneaking up behind him, Greg whipped around, but there was no one there. Perplexed, he stepped around the hedge, only to be pelted by six snowballs in a row right to the head.

"I surrender," he yelled, holding up his hands against the onslaught. "Stop! Ceasefire!"

"Do you acknowledge that I am the superior snowball fighter?" She was poised to throw another one, her arm cocked back menacingly. Or at least, it would be menacing if she wasn't grinning so hard.

"I was a fool to challenge you," he said, all the while backing toward his former hiding place.

"And you regret ambushing me under the guise of making a snowman, the most wholesome of all snow activities?"

"I do, of course." He hung his head, eyeing his stockpile.

She let her arm fall to her side, still clutching several snowballs. "Very well. I shall have pity on you. This time." When she turned toward the house, he dove for his stash and opened fire at her back.

Tharushi ducked out of the way at the other end of the hedge.

"You've betrayed me for the last time, Trout!" she hollered, and Greg threw back his head and laughed. He gathered up as many as he could, then snuck around the side. But she'd moved again, and he wound up chasing her back toward the garage, hardly hitting her at all. Now she was laughing, too. He caught her at the bottom of the stairs and wrapped his arms around her waist, pulling her against him.

"Don't," he gasped. "Don't run up the stairs, you'll fall."

"They're a death trap," she wheezed. Then she leaned back into his arms and let her head rest on his shoulder. All the words evaporated from his head. Greg squeezed her; on the one hand, it was unsatisfying, because their big puffy coats were between them, buffering the feel of her body against his, holding back her warmth. But on the other, he was holding the person he loved most in the world for the first time, and she'd started it. He held her, breathing in the cold with her, until she leaned forward.

"I should probably...get ready for work." She smoothed back her hair with her mittened hand.

"Yeah, me too. You go first. I'll be up in a minute."

She gave him a small smile before she turned and carefully made her way up the snowy steps. He watched her go, one step closer to making his decision.

GREG WENT AND CHECKED on Mrs. Foster first thing now when he arrived at work. The drive had been a little slippery, but nothing like the deep snow at home. Tharushi, however, had clung to the door handle and asked for more reassurances that he would get her to the airport. He didn't know where she'd disappeared to now.

"Good morning, Anne."

"Good morning, Dr. Trout." It was early enough that none of her friends had arrived yet to sit with her. "How was your weekend?"

He felt the heat rise in his cheeks. "It was nice. Really nice."

"Oh?" The older woman sat up a bit straighter in bed. "What was nice about it?"

He cleared his throat. "I spent some time with a friend."

"Come on, Dr. Trout, don't be shy. I'm stuck here in this bed. You might as well give me something interesting to think about."

He would absolutely not subject Tharushi to the rumor mill. The minute he mentioned her name, it would be all over town.

"How's your constipation this morning?"

"Don't change the subject."

"To be fair, this *is* the subject I came in here for..."

She crossed her arms stubbornly. "Can't an old woman want to hear a happy story at Christmastime?"

"I'll put on *It's a Wonderful Life* for you," he parried, getting out his stethoscope to listen to her heart and her lungs. She was quiet as he moved the bell around. Her lungs sounded clear enough.

"That movie's depressing," she said when he was done. "I'll take *Miracle on 34th Street*, though."

"Do you believe in Santa Claus, Mrs. Foster?"

"I don't want coal in my stocking, do I?"

He chatted with her more about her symptoms...she still wasn't sleeping well. The medication was helping, but not enough. Still felt slow mentally...it bothered him that there might not be much he could do about that. There had to be something more he could do. Treating her symptoms was important, but he wanted answers. If she had to spend the holidays in the hospital, she should get something out of that beyond an easier time in the bathroom.

He had her scoot to the edge of the bed and checked her reflexes. He tested her coordination, having her touch her nose with alternate hands. He checked her eye movement and sensation in her extremities.

"When can I get out of here? My family wants to come for Christmas, and I need to get ready."

He helped get her settled back onto the bed, then sighed. "I'm still concerned about your weight loss and your mental slowness. Is there anything else you can tell me about your condition? Anything you might have forgotten to mention?"

"Well, I took that fall..."

"Oh, right. Can you tell me more about that?"

Her shrug was weighted. "Not really. Just missed the next step, I guess. I don't like holding onto the railing."

He wrote that down and tried not to smirk. "Nothing loose? Carpet, boards?"

"I don't think so."

"Had it rained?"

"Nope, it was blessedly dry that day, that's why I was working out in the garden. Trying to divide my hostas before they completely took over." She rubbed at her forehead. "Hardly got out there again all summer, what with the trip to France and recovering from my injuries. But the Mind Readers took good care of me. That's my book group." Anne frowned. "Although I haven't actually read the book in quite some time. I guess I just go out of habit now."

"And we'd have it no other way."

Greg turned to see who was behind him and smiled at Hattie. "Good afternoon, Mayor."

"Not you, too," she said, rolling her eyes as she took off her hiking hat and sat down. "Speaking of, we'd like to have book group here next week, since it's our Christmas party."

"It'll have to be during visiting hours, but I see no reason why not, as long as everyone's healthy."

Hattie pointed at him as she turned to Anne. "Do you hear this? He wants us to be healthy before we come to the hospital. He's got it backward."

Greg chuckled and put away his pen and paper. "Just looking out for my patient. All right, Mrs. Foster, I'll see you later."

The two women began to discuss the snow with the excitement of children. But that nagging feeling that he was missing something followed him out of the room. He'd talk it over at their cohort meeting. They'd all figure it out.

CHAPTER
TWELVE

SHE'D ENDED UP WAITING for Greg to finish work, and rather than let the time go to waste, she snuck into the chapel. Letting her fingers wander over the cool keys had been therapeutic, as well as the few tears she'd allowed herself to spill. She'd just closed her eyes, letting the saltwater seal them, letting the music fill her senses instead. She loved Chopin's nocturnes, their fast-then-slow, romantic way, how the steadiness of the left hand let the right hand wander through the melody as if you really were on a moonlight path. The trills and up-and-down runs made it feel distinguished and orderly. C sharp minor, that was the right key for falling apart.

It hadn't been practical to get a piano here...electric pianos were terrible—no electronic noise could sufficiently soothe her soul—and she wasn't planning to be here long enough to accumulate belongings like that. So she settled for the one in the hospital's chapel when she was desperate enough to forego the privacy.

When they got home, all she wanted to do was eat and crawl into bed with a book, but they had that party to go to...Ainsley and Kyle's. Ainsley had come into the hospital today to see Winnie, and she did not look good. Maybe the party would get canceled? No. Wishful thinking. Tharushi would've heard by now. She usually didn't mind events like these, but the past few days had been a lot, and Greg was leaving soon, and...

Nope, she was going. He was going, so she'd go, too. Her bathroom door was open, which meant it was empty. She quickly stripped down and took a shower, rushing through her hair and makeup routines and grabbing her little black dress out of the closet.

Greg was standing in the living room, fiddling with his watch when she opened her door.

"Wow." He shoved his hands in his pockets. "Does it work on guys?"

"Does what work on guys?"

"Whatever you do in there." He turned and suddenly marched into the kitchen. "You worked a full day like I did, and I look rough. You look..."

"I look what?" It came out more prickly than she intended.

"Great!" he called, gathering up several plastic containers. Did his voice just crack? "You look great, is what I'm saying."

"Thanks." She smoothed down her dress; oh, the churned-up emotions were back. Too bad there was no piano here. "Ready to do our checklist?"

"Yep. And I've got the cookies."

"I've got your EpiPen."

"No tissues or gifts necessary...anything else?"

"I have my wallet in case you want to drink."

"Oh, okay. Thanks." He shrugged. "I think that's it, then. That felt too easy."

"Well, a Christmas party isn't a wedding. Maybe we don't need our checklist for smaller events."

"But I like our checklist," he protested as he got on his coat. Whatever he felt like, he didn't look rough to her. She'd seen him look a lot worse on overnight shifts. His mint green polo shirt and khakis were pleasantly festive, and paired with his brown leather coat, he looked perfect to her. He looked like himself.

They laughed and chatted about patients and the day's events on the way to the party, and she felt better when she got out of the car. Mostly. On the way up to the door, she took a deep breath and let it out slowly. She knew these people, and they knew her. Besides, she'd probably have to depend on them more once he was gone, so it made sense to deepen their relationships. She'd need some rides at the very least. *Rides...shoot, we still need to go car shopping.*

She took a breath to say so, but the door of the big white farmhouse opened.

"Hey, come on in, you guys," Daniel greeted. "They're in the kitchen."

"You're the wrong Durand. Am I at the right house?" Greg joked as they passed him.

"Like I'd know. I feel like I'm here as often as my house. You can toss your coats in the office to the left of the stairs." They came down the long hallway into the family room; four or five other people were milling around. Greg took her coat because he really was a gentleman, darn him, and Tharushi gravitated toward Trevor, one of the nurses, who was chatting with Maggie and Frankie.

"You get all those trees up okay?" Frankie asked, sipping a pink drink that matched her painted fingernails.

Tharushi nodded. "Well, someone did. They're up now and decorated, and they look great."

"My brothers made me help." Maggie rolled her eyes. "They have no sense of style."

"Yes, I do," Kyle protested from across the room. "I simply thought we would benefit from an artist's eye!"

"And they did," Tharushi agreed. "Far better than I could do."

"That must be why ours isn't decorated yet," Greg said as he came back to her side. "Not with the eighteen-hour shifts we worked."

"We should probably just pay Maggie to decorate ours," Tharushi said with a smile. "I'd sooner run fifteen miles." That reminded her of Mr. Oberst again and what she'd heard in the woods. She briefly considered bringing up his situation with her coworkers, but she still wasn't sure if it was her business.

"Twenty dollars an hour and you supply the decorations," Maggie deadpanned, and they all laughed.

"You want a drink?" Greg asked as the others spun off into a debate about Maggie's business practices.

She nodded. "You know what I like?" Tharushi asked, feeling unaccountably flirty. *Must be the mistletoe. Must resist Christmas spirit.*

"Sure do." Greg winked, and she smiled as she watched him go. When she turned back, Trevor and Maggie both looked ready to pounce.

"So what's your deal?" Maggie asked, her voice low.

Tharushi blinked, not understanding. "I beg your pardon?"

"You and Greg," Trevor said. "What's happening there?"

"Nothing's happening, we're roommates. We're friends."

"Just roommates?" Maggie's shoulders slumped. "When I saw you together at the tree farm, I thought for sure..." She sighed. "What a scam."

"How is that a scam?" Tharushi asked stiffly, wishing Greg would come back. Then again, it might make things more awkward if he knew they'd been talking about him.

"Just seems like he's pretty into you," Trevor said with a grin. "That's all. It's a shame to let all that pining go to waste."

"He's leaving anyway," Tharushi said.

"That's not what I heard," he said, lifting one eyebrow.

"What does that mean?" Tharushi asked, leaning closer. Is that what Greg had been so moody about lately? Trevor was well-known for his gossip, and she usually tried not to partake, but small towns seemed to take such things very seriously. *No, it's better to go to the source.* Without waiting for Trevor to answer, she turned and wove her way past her clustered colleagues into the small kitchen. But when she got there, her question died on her lips.

Greg was coughing, bent over with one hand on the counter, his face red. Kyle's wife Ainsley stood next to him, one hand on his shoulder, her face pinched with concern.

"Is he all right?"

Ainsley looked up, startled. "I don't know. He just started coughing and coughing. I patted him on the back, but it didn't seem to help."

Alarm rose in Tharushi. She rushed over to him, but he was staggering around the kitchen like he was drunk, and he seemed to be trying to get to the door. When she noticed her, he started putting his thumb up and down, like he was flipping an invisible coin.

"Was he eating anything? Drinking?"

"He had one of my almond cookies...but they're so small, I didn't think—"

She took Ainsley by the shoulders, not caring that she was frightening her. "What else is in them? Did they have sesame seeds?"

"Well, yes, they have tahini, but—"

Tharushi turned and darted for the office. *Not a coin—a pen.* She pawed through the giant pile of coats and purses until she found hers, hands shaking, and ran back to the kitchen, where by now a crowd had gathered.

"Get out of my way!" Her voice sounded cold as the winter wind, and people did as she commanded.

Kyle had Greg down on the ground, so it was easy to uncap the EpiPen and jab it into his leg. She knelt on the floor next to him, and when he turned his head and vomited, all she felt was relief. She put her hand on his chest and felt his breathing start to recover slowly; he locked his gaze on hers, and she didn't look away.

"Knew you'd figure it out," he wheezed, and he placed his hand over hers.

"THIS REALLY ISN'T NECESSARY," Greg complained as Tharushi dragged her down comforter and sheets into his room later that night.

"Lie down, please."

Greg sat up all the way because he was contrary and impossible. "How can I rest knowing you're sleeping on the floor?"

"Worry about yourself. Lie down and get some sleep. You need to recover," she said, gently pushing on his shoulders until he obeyed. As far as Tharushi was concerned, the most pointless thing she could do was try to sleep in her own room. She'd be straining her ears all night to hear him coughing or throwing up.

"Doctor, there's no reason to forfeit a good night's sleep. I'm fine. And you need to be rested for your flight home tomorrow." He was trying to be stern with her; it was so cute. How did this air mattress work, anyway? She turned it over, feeling around the edges until she found the valve to blow it up and inserted the pump like Kyle had shown her.

Greg sighed and sat up again. "You're really not going to sleep in your bed?"

"You're really not going to lie down?"

"Tharushi, be reasonable," he grumbled, pulling his covers up higher. "Have you even started packing?"

She might as well tell him. Then he could get a full night's sleep without worrying about an alarm in the morning. "I'm not going."

There was a beat where she thought he might not be upset after all.

"Like hell you're not."

Nope, that's what I thought would happen.

She ignored him. "I can delay my flight by a couple of days just to make sure you're all right."

"I *am* all right. I'm *fine.* Like I told you, all I need is a few hours' shut-eye, and I'll be good as gold. It's not that easy to rearrange travel plans around the holidays."

"Would you rather I take you back to Kyle's and let him watch over you tonight? That"s your other option. He did offer."

"No, I would rather we all sleep in our own beds and pack our own bags to take our own trips tomorrow!"

Tharushi got down on the floor and tested the air mattress with her hand. It seemed firm enough; it would do for one night. She set about putting her sheets on it.

"You are impossible to reason with," he grumped. "You're just—you're a bad listener."

"No, I'm a *great* listener. I just don't listen to BS."

"I'm not giving you BS!" he hollered, and Tharushi smiled.

"I bet you believe that. Now please lie down and go to sleep."

"You're getting on that flight tomorrow."

"We'll see how you're feeling."

He flopped backward, groaning. "Tharushi..."

"You know as well as I do that you could experience a recurrence of symptoms within a few hours. What are you going to do, stab yourself in the leg while your throat is closing? I don't think so."

That seemed to give him pause, and he rolled onto his side, propping his head in one hand. "I don't usually get rebound symptoms if that's what you're worried about. Seriously. You don't have to do this."

"Maybe I want to," she said quietly, as she focused on fluffing her pillow just right. "I'm going to put on my pajamas. You should turn out the light while I'm gone." She left his bedroom door as she moved back across the apartment; she had a pair of flannel pajamas that reminded her of something a nun would wear. Those would do the trick tonight. She quickly brushed her teeth and got the backup EpiPen they'd picked up at the hospital on their way home. Driving his truck in the snow had been nerve-wracking enough, but it was nothing like marching back across the apartment to see if he was going to throw another fit about her sleeping in his room. *Don't kick me out. Please don't. I can't take it. You were lying on the ground, flushed and sick, and if I hadn't been there...* Tharushi shut down the thought like she'd unplugged her brain. It wasn't going anywhere; she *had* been there. She'd helped him. And if not, he was in a room full of medical professionals who would've figured it out quickly enough. And yet...

To her great relief, his light was off, and he was lying on his back, unmoving enough to be asleep. She crept across the creaky floor and slipped under the cold covers. This close to the floor, she could feel the cold seeping up from the garage; it wasn't well insulated. It was going to be a long night. Tharushi tried to pull the covers up higher over her shoulders, but she stilled when he rolled over.

"Peaches?" he whispered, his voice still raspy from all the coughing earlier.

"Yes?"

"Is there anything I can say to get you to go back to your room? You can't be comfortable down there."

"Life isn't all about comfort. Also, no."

Greg sighed, and she heard him roll onto his back again. "You're stubborn."

She chuckled. "You're just now figuring this out?"

"No," he said softly, "I knew it before. Anyone else would've quit."

"Quit trying to convince you to let me sleep on your floor?"

"No, quit the hospital. It's been a hard two years."

"It has," she admitted. On the ceiling, the reflected snow was lighting up the room a little, but it was dark enough and she was tired, so the truth came easier. "I wouldn't have made it without you."

"Oh, sure you would—"

"No, Greg. I wouldn't. Without the driving and the meals and just...companionship. I would've given up."

"No, you're stronger than that. You're the strongest person I know. You'd have found a way."

"Maybe."

Quiet fell between them. Shadows moved on the ceiling, and she knew it was snow falling past the lights that bracketed the driveway outside. *More snow.* Even if he was feeling better tomorrow, would he be able to get them to the airport? People here didn't know how to drive in the snow; they were constantly sliding into things, thinking their four-wheel-drive would somehow make them immune to icy conditions. *Boneheads.*

"Why do you hate it here?"

She thought for a moment. "I don't *hate* it—"

"I know you do. I know you miss Chicago like crazy."

Tharushi pushed her hair away from her face. "I guess it's just not what I'm used to."

"Even after all this time?"

She shrugged, even though he couldn't see her. "Not what I prefer is more accurate, I guess."

"I'm glad you didn't quit." His voice was low and scratchy, and she couldn't tell if it was emotion or just fatigue from the day. "You helped me, too. That's why I can't let you miss out on this chance for my sake. I'll call my mom, and she'll send one of my sisters down to drive with me. Please. Don't stay here just for me. Go see your family."

"We'll see how you're feeling. Let's get some sleep."

"Okay." Greg finally sounded resigned, but she couldn't feel happy about it. *He doesn't want me to stay for him, and that's all I want to ask him to do for me. To stay.* She hadn't ever gotten to ask him about Trevor's comment...was he really thinking about staying? What would he do here? All he'd ever talked about was going back to Bluewater, even if he didn't seem very excited about it sometimes. *Why would he stay?* In a tiny, neglected corner of her heart, Tharushi could feel a spark; that curious question flickered, into an idea, and then a wish, and then a hope. That he was staying for her. Not just because they were friends and because he needed her, too...but because he wanted more.

The sheets were warm now, trapping her body heat inside. His breathing was steady and slow, but she couldn't see if he was lying there awake, too. She picked up her phone.

> **Amma:** We will pick you up tomorrow at baggage claim. We are all coming.

> **Tharushi:** I might not make it. Greg had a bad allergic reaction.

> **Amma:** Ai ya. I'm sorry. He's okay now?

> **Tharushi:** I think so. But I want to be sure.

Amma: Is there no one else to care for him?

Tharushi: Amma, it's just not right to shove him off on someone else. He's my friend.

Amma: But maybe he has other friends, no? Friends who don't have an important flight to catch.

Tharushi: Amma. Don't be selfish.

Amma: I want to see my daughter for Christmas. Is that selfish? We have given them so much, we have given you to them for so long. Someone else can take a turn.

Tharushi: I will do my best to be there, but I'm not leaving him if he's still sick.

There was a long pause, and she knew Amma was probably talking to Appaa. They were good at talking sense into each other most of the time. Kind of like someone else she knew...

Amma: Okay, diyaṇiya. You are a good friend. Just promise us you will try your best to come soon.

Tharushi: Yes, I promise. Good night.

Amma: Good night.

Tharushi shoved her phone under the pillow. Greg was quiet and still above her, and she wanted to stand up so she could see his face, but she was afraid the floor would creak and wake him up. Her phone let out of a triplet of muffled buzzes, and it was a bit of a surprise who it was.

Aruj: You're bagging on Christmas?
Pradeep: We haven't seen you in forever!
Ravi: No one can cover for you with this patient?

Amma must have stretched the truth a little...interesting. It was nice of her, actually—her brothers would tease her mercilessly if they knew who she was really staying for.

Tharushi: It's not a sure thing yet. We'll see how he's doing in the morning.

Ravi: I found a flight that leaves later. You should rebook it now before it fills up.

Aruj: Seconded.

Pradeep: Or there's always a train if the planes are full.

Aruj: Uh, only if she wants to get here by New Year's. Driving would be faster.

Ravi: She can't drive halfway across the country by herself. Maybe one of us could fly out and drive with her.

Pradeep: I'm not trying to be a jerk, but can she even drive? Tharushi, can you drive?

Aruj: Of course she can drive!

Pradeep: Then how come she never got a car? She said she was going to.

Ravi: Her roommate shares his, I believe. Or he drives her, I'm not sure which.

Tharushi: 1. I CAN drive. 2. I will FLY to Chicago when my patient is better, probably tomorrow. 3. GOOD NIGHT.

She jammed the phone under the pillow, annoyed. She hadn't heard from them in weeks, and now they wanted to blow up her phone in the middle of the night? Okay, it was only 9:30. But it was later there. What were they still doing up? The buzzing had stopped, and she tried to close her eyes, but sleep wouldn't come. If she was in her room, she'd be reaching for her Bluetooth headphones and scrolling to another nocturne. But here, she was alone with her thoughts, stuck in the silence for her "patient's" sake.

"Greg?" she whispered.

There was no response. Tharushi swallowed hard, but her heart wouldn't let her hold back the words any longer. It would not be ignored tonight.

"You were right," she whispered. "I do hate it here. Or at least, I did before you helped me get used to it. I'm so scared that I can't do this without you. That the last two years will be for nothing. That when you're gone, what little joy I had here will be gone, too. I need you. I wish you'd stay. I know it's selfish, and that's why I can't ask you, but I want to so much. I..."

The words finally petered out. Because even if he was asleep, she could not profess her love. That was a secret she'd kept even from herself until that moment, watching the shadows swim like fish on the ceiling above her. It was a peaceful revelation, in some ways—for a long time, she'd considered herself incapable of that kind of affection. The kind of strong romantic feelings that came so easily to others had felt out of her reach. She'd had relationships with other people, even physical ones. But they never evoked that kind of deep longing she'd expected. They were...bland. Letting them go hadn't been difficult. But for Greg? There wasn't much she wouldn't do, and his face was familiar and safe, and they *knew* each other. And that was enough.

"I love you." The words were so quiet, the breath of them barely passed over her lips. And finally, having relieved her burdened soul to her unconscious roommate, she fell asleep.

CHAPTER
THIRTEEN

GREG WOKE TO THE SMELL of coffee. He rolled to one side; she was gone. The air mattress and her sheets were still there in a messy pile. His door was closed. He looked toward the window—the white snow was blinding. He cursed softly. If it was light out, that meant...he jumped out of bed and threw on his jeans and a sweatshirt. Maybe they could still make her flight if he hurried...he felt okay. A little tired, but he'd slept well. And coffee would help.

He whipped open the door and jumped when she was standing right in front of it.

"Good morning," she said with an unnatural amount of cheer.

"Did we miss it?"

"The flight I moved to the afternoon? No, we still have plenty of time."

His stomach clenched. "But you had to pay a big change fee, didn't you?"

She took a sip of her coffee, a black curl sliding out of her ponytail as she nodded.

"I'll pay you back," he said quickly. "I'm sorry. You should've woken me up, you should've..."

Tharushi smirked at him over the rim of her mug. "You established a 'no repayment' policy when we moved in. I tried to get you that gift card..."

"No, no. That was totally different. That was something neighbors do for each other, and you..."

"Sleeping your floor so you don't die in the night is *not* something neighbors do for each other? Wow. Even us city folk would do that. Maybe it's something doctors do for each other."

A smile tugged at his lips, but he wiped it off when he ran a hand down his face. "You can't be my doctor."

She lowered her mug and pushed her shoulders back indignantly. "Why not?"

"We *live* together. And I heard you bellow at all our coworkers last night, so don't tell me you're objective. Not with a room-clearing shout like that."

She was grinning at him, and he wanted to tuck that loose curl behind her ear and pull her close and kiss the smile from her face. Greg cleared his throat, then frowned. It was still sore from the vomiting he'd done yesterday.

"What time do we need to leave?"

"Around nine. It's seven now." She was watching him carefully, and the smile had disappeared. "How are you feeling?"

He leaned closer with a smirk. "I told you, I'm fine. Thanks to you."

Tharushi lifted one hand, then hesitated. "Can I..."

"Yes."

Her smile was back. "You didn't let me finish."

"I don't need to. I trust you."

The soft look in her eyes was one he hadn't seen often; the last time her mom left was the only one recently. Tharushi pressed the inside of her wrist to his forehead.

"No fever."

"Nope." That wouldn't make any sense, but he didn't mention it.

"How's your stomach?"

He put a hand to it, as if that would help him determine what was going on down there. "Okay, I think? Probably need to put something into it to know for sure."

"But you're not nauseated?" she asked, leading the way toward the kitchen.

"Not at the moment."

"Here." She held out a steaming mug. "I heard you get up, so I made you some peppermint tea."

"How festive."

She elbowed him gently enough that she didn't slosh the hot liquid. "It's a natural remedy for stomach problems."

"But I don't have a stomach problem," he said, taking a small sip. There were undernotes of something else in there besides peppermint, something earthy. "I had an allergic reaction to a food I can't tolerate. Now I'm better."

"Who puts tahini into a Christmas cookie?" Tharushi grumped, and Greg smiled.

"I know, right?" She hadn't yelled at him at all for not being careful, which he appreciated. He was very careful; this was the first time he'd needed an EpiPen since he moved here. "I didn't even think to ask. What's in this?"

"Oh, green tea, too. Antioxidants are good."

"Yes. Okay. I should pack."

Her eyes widened. "You're still driving to Bluewater to-day?"

He shrugged. "Yeah. I mean, I might pull over and take a nap along the way, but..."

Her scowl was deep. "Can't you just go tomorrow?"

"Traffic will be better today. And I'm already headed in the right direction when I drop you off."

"You're an hour and a half into an eight-hour drive."

"If I drop you off at ten thirty, I'll get there before bedtime. Besides, I don't drive the speed limit when I get out into the middle of nowhere, so it's more like seven." He winked, but she just crossed her arms. "No, Tharushi-bot," he gasped, "not stubborn mode!"

"We'll check the highway cameras and see if it's clear." Without asking permission, she turned and went over to his laptop, which still sat open and on from yesterday.

"Okay, but I'm gonna need to pack that in a few minutes."

She gave him a thumbs-up without looking at him. She was...different? More open? It was like someone had taken the hairline crack in her walls he usually tried to peek through and put a crowbar in it. He didn't know how or why, but he was enjoying it. He'd enjoy it right up until he had to say goodbye to her. After Christmas, they'd only have a few days together, and he'd spend most of that packing and working. *If I'm moving after all...*maybe he'd have time to think about the job on the drive.

Her voice jarred him from his thoughts. "Are you going 97?"

"No, they don't like speeding on the reservation. I'll go through Kennewick. It'll have less snow, anyway." He stood in his doorway, just watching her read. He didn't want to pack. Greg turned and got out his phone to search "vacation packing list" on the internet. Someone out there would tell him what to bring.

Ninety minutes later, having reclaimed his laptop and gathered the essentials, they met by the front door.

"Got your ticket?" he asked, his heart heavy.

She nodded. "Wallet and keys?"

He held them up. "Got your ID? Presents? Warm coat?"

"Yes, yes, and yes. Do you have your EpiPen?"

"Uh..." *Shoot.* When he picked up her sheets and stuff, he'd seen it on the ground. He must have kicked it under the bed and forgotten about it. "I'll be right back."

"Seriously, Greg?" she called after him. "This is not inspiring confidence!"

He knelt, and sure enough, there it was. "I'm fine, I just forgot! You stole it last night, that's why."

"Oh, yes. Blame me."

"I do," he said with a sniff. "All right. Let's get this show on the road." It took a bit of wrestling to get everything into the back seat; he'd planned to put his stuff in the bed, but it was wet. Finally, they were on the road. He took it slow down their driveway, but once they were out on the road, it was mostly just wet pavement with a few slick spots in the shade. The radio was already on Christmas music, so he left it there, even if the idea of Mommy kissing Santa Claus was putting other ideas in his head.

They chatted the way good friends do: they recounted silly moments from their history, teased each other about their idiosyncrasies, and speculated about their patients and coworkers.

To his relief, she didn't turn the conversation toward the future, and it was easy to give himself permission not to think about it for a while. But he was still thinking about her. How he wanted to tell her how he felt before it was too late. When he'd have to try to do it over the phone like a coward, or when he was about to leave to move back to Bluewater, also like a coward. If he told her now, she'd have time to think about it while they were apart. And he'd have the information he needed to make his decision.

"Feeling okay?" Tharushi's face was pinched again.

"Yup!" he said. But he was almost out of time, so at the last moment, he turned toward the parking garage.

"You're not just dropping me?"

"No, I'll help you get your stuff inside."

"You don't have to…" she argued, but it was too late anyway. Yeah, it would cost him four bucks, but it gave him another few minutes to get his courage together.

Come on, Trout. You can do this. Just open your mouth and say, "I like you a lot. I think you're a sensitive, intuitive person, and a delightful, supportive colleague, and a fun, beautiful friend, and a bunch of other things I can't think of because I'm nervous as heck. If I stayed, could we give dating a shot?" That doesn't sound too bad. He practiced in his head a few more times as they rolled her maroon suitcases across the open-air bridge from the parking garage to the terminals. But as they waited to check her in, shuffling forward at intervals, his brain started unhelpfully thinking about what she might say in response.

I thought you were moving back to Bluewater?
Why didn't you tell me you had a job offer?
How long have you felt this way?

Why would you think I *felt that way?*

It was her turn, and he lifted one of her bags onto the scale while she got out her ID. He gave the attendant a tight smile and nodded along as she made polite small talk with them. Finally, they handed her the boarding pass, and Tharushi led the way toward the security checkpoint. He pulled her to the side by a restaurant with a tropical theme called Beaches.

"I'll see you in a few days," she said, glancing toward the growing line.

"Yeah. Hope you have a good Christmas." *Tell her. Say it. Just do it.*

"Yes, you too." The phone in her hand started to ring, and she answered it. "Hi, Amma. No, I'm not at my gate yet, but there's plenty of time." She rolled her eyes, and he chuckled nervously. "Yes, much better, he's just dropping me off." She was looking toward security again, and he knew she was anxious to go. He'd heard these Amma conversations go on a long time. Greg's cheeks heated, disappointment searing his insides, and he jammed his hands into his pockets sheepishly as he turned to go.

"Hang on, Amma. Hang on one second."

He could hear her mom still talking through the phone as Tharushi nabbed his coat sleeve and pulled him into a hug. Greg wrapped his arms around her slowly, like he wasn't sure this wasn't a trick. But all signs pointed to it being real, from the scent of her expensive salon shampoo and the tickle of her curly hair against his cheek to the sound of her breath in his ear and the way she squeezed him a little as she let go.

"Drive safe," she whispered, holding the phone away from her mouth. "Text me when you get there."

Greg managed a nod even though his brain was scrambled and useless, as she grabbed her carry-on with one hand and lengthened her stride to get in front of a large group of teenagers in matching red sweatshirts. He stood there, watching her talk to her mom until she got her shoes back on. She waved, and he waved back.

And he was fairly sure he floated back to his truck.

CHAPTER FOURTEEN

THE PLANE BUMPED ALONG the taxiway at O'Hare, and Tharushi breathed a sigh of relief. Her flight had been delayed over an hour because of the weather, but she'd made it. The minute the flight attendants authorized the use of cell phones again, Tharushi powered hers on to read the message she knew was waiting for her.

> **Greg:** Made it to Bluewater. Felt weird to drive around without you in my truck.

Tharushi smiled and checked her watch. He had made good time, like he'd said.

> **Tharushi:** Say hi to your mom for me.
> **Greg:** Will do. Say hi to your family from me, too.

Tharushi gave him a thumbs-up. She wanted to do more, but she'd had to upgrade to first class to get on this flight, so she didn't have to wait to disembark. *Definitely not going to mention that to Greg if he tries to pay me back again.* It wasn't a problem; her dad would pay her back. They just wanted her home.

Home. A blast of dry, cold air hit her as she stepped into the jetway, and she smiled. Oregon was so much wetter; she'd need to remember to use lotion here. She wound her way through O'Hare wishing she'd worn running shoes instead of her boots, but she'd been worried they'd get stuck in the snow and she'd have to help push or something. It was busy—holiday travel was the worst. But when she rounded the corner and saw Appaa and Amma and all three of her brothers clustered together, talking and laughing, her heart swelled.

"There she is!" Pradeep, her next oldest brother, spotted her first and came loping over on his long legs. His black hair was cut short so it didn't curl, and he engulfed her in a hug. Ravi and Aruj weren't far behind, and soon, she was being squished by everyone.

"Can't breathe," she quipped, and they laughed as they let her go. But Amma kissed her on both cheeks as the guys wandered over to the carousel to watch for her luggage.

"Have you eaten? I made kottu roti."

"They gave me food in first class," she answered, enjoying just looking at her mom's face. She looked older: there were more lines around her eyes, and she was positive she hadn't had that much gray in her hair the last time they'd been together.

"You look tired. Did you sleep on the plane?"

"A little bit." The first hour, she'd stared out the window and second-guessed that hug. But then she watched a movie, during which she fell asleep and now could never know the ending unless she spent money to watch it. Terrible. "I didn't sleep well last night." She decided to omit the part about being in Greg's room since she knew her parents hadn't been totally comfortable with the whole male roommate situation in the first place. He'd done his best to win her mom over the first time she came to visit, though, and now Amma was a big fan of the man. As a roommate, anyway...

"This is yours, yes?" Appaa held up her big maroon suitcase, and Thaurshi nodded.

"Your uncle Bashitha and auntie Jagathi came in this morning," Amma went on. "Your cousin Danara, she's getting married in the summer, and they want you to come."

"Here in Chicago?" Ravi took her carry-on from her with a smile and gave her another side hug.

"No, in Atlanta."

"I don't know if I'll be able to get the time off, but I'll try."

Amma's mouth did that thing she hated, pressed into a flat line of displeasure. It was too late to argue with her. Tharushi allowed herself to be ushered to the car, and Pradeep squeezed into the back with the other two seats put down for her suitcases. She was flanked on the middle bench seat with Ravi on her left and Aruj on her right.

"How's your patient?" Ravi asked as Appaa pulled out of the parking garage.

"Better," she said. "Thanks for asking."

"I didn't know Dr. Trout had food allergies," Amma said with the utmost innocence in her voice. Ah, so it wasn't that she wanted to cover for her; she just wanted to toss that information in like a grenade and watch the guys explode.

"Wait, *another doctor* was your patient? Is that legal?"

"How would they ever get better if it was?" Pradeep was ridiculous sometimes.

"Is Greg all right?" Ravi asked, clearly concerned.

"Yes, he's okay now."

"Who's Greg?" Aruj was the least tuned into her life.

"Her roommate," Ravi said. Her biggest brother was almost like a second dad, and as such, he was scowling. "They've lived together for two years. How do you not know his name?"

"It's not like she tells us anything about her life..." Aruj grumbled.

"Well, that's true," said Pradeep.

"I tell Ravi things. You two never answer my emails."

"Who uses email?" they both said at the same time, and Tharushi and Ravi shared a look at their expense.

"Come to think of it," Aruj said, rubbing his chin thoughtfully, "I have heard her talk about her roommate before. In fact, it's all I ever hear her talk about." Her middle brother had always been a pot-stirrer.

"Me too. I didn't know his name, but she talks about him a *lot*." If she could have reached Pradeep, she would've smacked him for keeping this going. Nicely, of course.

"Of course I do. We live together and work together."

"And you stayed in Oregon for him?" Pradeep said. "Interesting..."

"It's not interesting. It's not even noteworthy. He was sick. Who else was going to take care of him?" She did not want to talk about this with them, not when her mind was still turning things over. It was another twenty minutes back into the city; at least the traffic was light at this time of night.

"What's he like? You know, besides being allergic to stuff."

"Like, how tall is he?" Tharushi snarked. "He's only allergic to sesame seeds, as far as I know."

"Yeah, I want to know about this guy, too," Pradeep called. "What kind of stuff does he like?"

"He's forgetful." *Which is why we have our checklist routine.* "His style is basic." *But I definitely have a preference about what he wears, because I'm kind of in love with him.* "He likes walking in the woods." *And he comes back with rain in his hair and his cheeks glowing pink and he looks so happy.* "And *M*A*S*H*." *Which is terrible Asian representation, but we've talked about it and both acknowledge it was a product of the times.*

"Harsh," Aruj muttered. Yeah, without the rest of her thoughts, it probably did sound kind of rude.

"Dr. Trout is a very nice man," Amma put in sharply from the front seat. "He took me to a very nice vegetarian restaurant in a nearby city, and he treats Tharushi with great respect. That is all you need to know."

Thanks, Amma. Silence fell over the occupants of the car for about sixty seconds.

"So you like him?" Aruj prompted. "You do, don't you?"

She groaned. "Be a grown-up, ayiya."

"She likes him! Tharushi's in looooovvee," Pradeep called.

"All of you back there, shut up, I'm trying to drive," Appaa exclaimed from the front seat. That ended that conversation for good until they pulled up in front of the red rowhouse. Tharushi dragged herself into the house and collapsed onto the sofa, which was a mistake for two reasons: it was comfortable, so her body announced that it wasn't getting up again. Also, her parents' Pomeranian Coco jumped up on the couch next to her, white fluffy tail going wild, and she spent the next few minutes consoling him.

By the time she stood up, her father and brothers had already carried her stuff upstairs. At least she'd have privacy up there; being the only girl, she had her own room. She was almost there when Ravi appeared in the hallway.

"Hey."

"Yes?"

"Do you like him, though?"

Tharushi hesitated. She glanced up and down the hall, but it seemed like there was no one around, and this was Ravi. He was dependability itself.

"Yeah."

"I knew it!" Aruj crowed, sticking his head out of their bedroom. "Ha! Who called it?"

Ravi pushed him back into the bedroom and held the door shut despite his brother's protests. "Are you dating?"

"No. He's leaving, anyway...I think."

"The internet is a thing. You could do long-distance. Knowing you, you'd prefer it."

"What's that supposed to mean?" she hissed, and Ravi grinned.

"Just that you like your privacy. That's all." She couldn't really argue with that. Maybe it didn't matter if he left. They had two years together to draw from, a solid foundation of friendship and trust.

"But I like him, too. I don't need as much space from him as I do from other people, usually. I don't know how that would feel."

"So find out. What do you have to lose?"

So much. A colleague. A confidant. My closest friend.

"When did you become such an expert on love?" she deadpanned. Tharushi heard someone coming up the stairs with heavy footfalls, and she turned.

"If you don't go to sleep," Appaa intoned somberly, "Santa won't come."

When Tharushi gave them both a big hug, they looked surprised. She didn't know why she was so into hugging lately. Apparently, the stress was finally getting to her. Tharushi whispered 'good night' to both of them and went into her bedroom, shutting the door quietly. The ancient digital clock by the bed read 12:13 a.m., and she rubbed blearily at her forehead. She dug out her phone charger and collapsed into bed...but not before sending one more message.

Tharushi: Merry Christmas, Greg.

CHAPTER
FIFTEEN

GREG'S FINGERS WERE already stiff with cold as he entered the barn in the dim light of sunrise. His mom sat on the three-legged wooden stool, humming to herself, her hands working steadily to relieve Grace of her milk.

"Should've known I couldn't beat you," he said, a rueful smile crossing his face. She glanced at him over her shoulder with a smile.

"Why'd you try, then?"

"Because it's Christmas, Mom. I wanted to do something nice for you."

"You did," she said, lifting her gaze to him as he came to stand next to her. "You came home."

"That wasn't a hardship. You know that."

"Keep me company, then." She paused to pull out another stool for him, and he sat down. Her gaze was assessing as it passed over his face. "How are you feeling today?"

"Just fine." That early morning text from Tharushi had certainly given him plenty to smile about.

"Sounds like we were lucky Dr. Udawatte was there."

"Yup," he said softly. The tickle in his nose was just from the hay; there was nothing to feel emotional about. They'd been apart *one day*. Not even a whole day yet.

His mom chuckled. "Boy, you've got it bad."

"You can tell that from one word?" he grumped, shoving his hands deeper into his pockets.

"No, I can tell that from how your eyes got soft and you looked lonely even though we're sitting here together." She pulled a handkerchief out of the pocket of her thick brown Carhartt coat; it used to be his dad's. But she had more use for it the past few years. His mom eyed him as she dabbed at her runny nose. "You going to deny you're in love with her?"

"Mom..." He sighed. "It's not that simple. I promised Dr. H I'd come home. Tharushi, she's..." He sighed again. "Well, she's not done with her internship for one thing. And then she has her cardiac internship somewhere else. But she doesn't like small towns. She misses Chicago."

"Maybe she'll miss you more."

"Not too likely. You don't know how much she hates it in Oregon."

His mom cocked her head. "I thought it was nice. I liked it."

"So do I! And they offered me this job at Santiam..."

"Oh, really?" She sat up. "What did you tell them?"

"That I needed time to think about it." He scooped up some straw and rubbed it between his fingers. It was soft and almost silky, and it reminded him of Tharushi's hair brushing against him when she'd given him that hug.

"Gregory Alan Trout."

Uh oh. Whenever she pulled out his full name, he knew he was about to get an earful. Even though he was thirty now, it still made him feel more like thirteen.

"Yes, ma'am?"

"If there's a job available in a town where the person you're interested in pursuing lives, why wouldn't you take it?"

"Because I promised..." he mumbled, but he cut himself off when he met her sympathetic gaze.

"Mom!" Flora stuck her head into the barn, braiding her hair off to one side. "How long do the cinnamon rolls rise? I can't find the recipe..."

"Be right there," she called back. His mom stood with a quiet groan, one hand supporting her back.

"I'll finish up out here. You go inside," he said, urging her toward the door.

"All right." She wagged a finger at him. "But we're going to finish this conversation later."

"Yes, ma'am." The other cows, Faith and Hope, took longer than he thought to finish; they were good girls and stood still for him, but he was out of practice. He took the milk back to the house with him, sniffling from the cold just like his mom had been.

"Thank you." June opened the door for him as he came up the steps. "You can leave it on the porch. Lynne wants to make peppermint ice cream later and there's no room in the fridge anyway."

"Plenty cold out here," he said, stamping his feet as he came inside. "I've spent too much time on the west side. I'm not used to it anymore."

"Getting soft down there in Oregon, eh?" June laughed.

"Guess so," he said. "Is there coffee?"

"Here you go," his dad called, wheeling down the hall, mug in hand. "Saw you coming and you looked cold."

"Thanks, Dad." Greg took the cup gratefully and let it warm his freezing hands for a moment before he took a sip. "You ready to do this?"

"Definitely." Walt grinned. "I've got a good feeling you're going to like my gift." Greg followed him into the living room where Flora, Lynne, and Mom were all waiting patiently to open stockings. June came rushing in behind him. The tree was all lit up, presents piled high under it, and their cat Rascal was asleep underneath it. It was silly to call them stockings, he mused as he sat down. They were huge, not even remotely the size of a regular sock, and they were still overflowing with small tissue-wrapped packages. His mom had color-coded all of them. Where did she find the time to do all this? His dad had a caregiver who helped him with personal hygiene and such, but she still ran the household and the farm.

As soon as his dad got into his chair, the free-for-all began. The frivolous things were on top: his favorite candy (Christmas M&M's—the red and green made them more fun than the regular ones), a gift card for Riverside (had Mom gotten it when she came to town? Sneaky.), honey, and jam from Made in Washington. Then toward the middle, he started hitting the practical things: a new toothbrush ("to get rid of all that sugar on your teeth"), pocket-size hand sanitizer, wool socks ("I knit those," Flora whispered with a grin.), natural bug repellent for his forest walks, his favorite cologne. Greg sat back and listened to the radio playing jazzy Christmas standards, watching his family.

It was hard to imagine Tharushi here...she'd probably be embarrassed to open gifts in front of everyone. And yet, he could imagine her tucked into his side, whispering inside jokes to each other. Going for walks around the farm to get space from everyone else. It could be good. His sisters would like her.

June sat down next to him. "You good?"

"Yeah. Just thinking."

"But you're feeling okay? You scared the crap out of us."

"Sorry. Didn't expect Christmas cookies to have sesame products."

She rolled her eyes. "Everybody's gotta be gourmet these days."

Greg snorted. "Yeah, I guess so. Ainsley's kind of an over-achiever. It shouldn't surprise me."

June scooted closer and put her head on his shoulder, and he smiled. "It's nice to see my big brother."

"It's nice to see you, too."

"We're looking forward to having you closer to home. Did you hear there's a spot opening up at the high school for me next year?"

"Really?"

"Yup. As soon as I graduate, it's mine. Tenth grade math. Algebra I and Geometry."

"Juney, that's fantastic." He pivoted to give her a crushing hug, cursing himself internally. Why couldn't he be like June, happy to come back to Bluewater? Dedicated to what he said he would do? Wasn't it enough to know that he was supporting his community? What was it all for if he just stayed in Timber Falls?

"What's that look for?" June was staring at him quizzically.

"Nothing." He smiled. No reason to ruin her holiday with his problems. "Just thinking."

"Doing a lot of that today…"

"A disadvantage of downtime," he joked. "I'm gonna get more coffee. You want some?"

"No, I'm good."

"You sure? I need you sharp for making that ice cream later. My belly is counting on it."

June rolled her eyes at him and waved him off. "You'll get some, don't you worry."

By the time Greg came back with his coffee, June had vacated the couch and Lynne was in her place. She held up a deck of cards, and he grinned. Before breakfast was ready, she'd trounced him twice at gin rummy. He stuffed himself silly with cinnamon rolls, egg-and-bacon casserole, and fruit salad. He was just polishing off his third roll, licking his sticky fingers when the front door opened.

"Merry Christmas, all," said a familiar voice, and Greg's head snapped up. He jumped up from the table, hastily rubbing his hands on his jeans, then offered his hand to Dr. Hernández.

"Merry Christmas, sir. This is a surprise."

"Yes, I imagine," the older man said through a chuckle. "Do you have a minute to talk?"

He blinked at him, confused. "Um…" He looked to his mom and dad, who both nodded.

"We'll wait for you," Dad said, handing him his coat and shoes. Greg narrowed his eyes at him and his mom suspiciously, but they just smiled at him.

"Great," Dr. H said, clapping his hands. "We won't be long. Let's go for a walk."

Greg followed him outside and down the front steps, breathing on his hands before he shoved them into his lined pockets. He lengthened his stride to walk next to him. He hadn't changed much since he'd last seen him: same ears that stuck out a bit too much from a thin brown face, white mustache, same tan cap he usually wore. But his pace was slower, his shoulders more hunched, and his hands shook a little bit as he zipped up his coat.

"It's good to see you, Greg. I get regular updates on you from your dad at the men's group at church, of course. But it's not the same as the real thing. Tell me about..." He paused like he was mentally searching for the name of the hospital.

"Santiam," Greg supplied. "It's good. It's different than here. It's still rural, but Salem is kind of like their Chewelah if we have problems...and then Portland is right there if we need to refer them. Kind of like their Spokane." He scratched his head. "Now that I think about it, maybe it's not that different from here."

Dr. H smiled. "How's the administration at the hospital? I remember when I was living in Yakima..." He spun off into a story, and they traded them back and forth for a few minutes until they got to the end of their long driveway. Dr. H turned around, then paused. "I guess I should tell you why I'm here. Your dad called me."

"I *knew* it." Greg sighed, but Dr. H put a hand on his shoulder.

"Don't be upset with him. He's right; you have a good thing going in Timber Falls. It sounds like you're happy there?"

Greg felt his eyebrows form a deep V. "Yes, I'm happy there, but it was never meant to be permanent..."

His mentor laughed. "What's permanent? You know what they say—you want to make God laugh, tell him your plans." He let his hand drop. "I never meant to stay here long. It was a job, and I needed one, and then I met Maritza, and well…" He grinned. "The rest, as they say, is history. So I understand changing plans. Maybe after another year there…"

"It's three years. She's in cardiology."

Dr. H's smile didn't waver. "So you're telling me I could have two doctors for the price of one? Hot damn."

Frustrated, Greg shook his head. "You're putting the cart before the horse here, Doc. I'd have to ask her out first." The thought made his heart thump painfully.

"Would she say yes?"

"I don't know!" Greg shouted, then immediately felt terrible. "I'm sorry. I don't mean to take it out on you…it's just, I've been wrestling with this for days and I don't have any answers and I don't know what to do!" He ran a hand through his unbrushed hair. "I made you a promise. I told you I'd come back so you could retire, and now…"

"And now another life is calling to you. Another adventure."

Greg met his sympathetic gaze and, to his embarrassment, felt hot tears rolling down his cold cheeks as he nodded.

"The beautiful thing about being a doctor is that everyone's got a body," Dr. H said lightly. "So you'll be needed anywhere you want to be. Sounds like you just need to decide where that is. Don't feel obligated to come and take my job. I wouldn't be able to live with myself if you gave up something special with your friend for my sake. We'll figure something out. There's some rural physician groups that might be able to help."

Greg knew he should feel free, relieved. But he didn't. Because he knew that doctors who wanted to come live in the middle of nowhere just weren't that easy to find. Even if he did find someone to take the job, would he ever have peace about breaking his promise? Integrity was important to him.

"Well, I appreciate your graciousness, sir."

They started back toward the house in silence, the wind whipping across their faces.

"I can't believe you came out here on Christmas," Greg said, kicking at the gravel.

"Doctors work every day of the year. You know that." Dr. H was quiet for a moment. "I opened my new golf clubs first. I'm gonna go try them out on my way home."

"Well, that's a consolation, anyway. Thanks for coming by. You should have some peppermint ice cream if it's ready."

His eyes lit. "Homemade?"

"You know it."

"God bless Lynne."

CHAPTER SIXTEEN

IT WAS THE DAY AFTER Christmas, and Tharushi was holding an inordinate amount of shopping bags. Part of her Christmas gift had been gift cards to go to the Miracle Mile with her mom, Auntie Jagathi, and her cousins. Her dad said it was because they all needed "girl time." Secretly, she believed he valued a quiet house after a day of hubbub and loud voices. But she didn't mind claiming a few new outfits in the interest of family peace.

"So you're a doctor now, kasin akka?" Sunila was only sixteen, so it wasn't surprising that she looked up to her.

"Yes, technically," Tharushi said, touching the fabric of a petal pink pashmina she thought her mom would like.

"That's so amazing! I want to try to go into medicine. But probably not a doctor; nursing doesn't take as long."

"Nurses are just as important," Tharushi affirmed. "Have you looked into any programs yet? UIC used to have a good program..." When she'd started college...over a decade past. How was it so long ago?

"Just a little bit." She glanced over her shoulder at Tharushi's mom and auntie, chatting over by the purses. "I was thinking of California. Just to, you know, have a little space. Date whoever I want."

Tharushi gave her a curt nod. "That is a nice luxury. But after a while, you might miss them more than you think."

Sunila's eyes widened. "You don't like Oregon?" She thought for a minute, rifling through some belts. They were too flashy for her taste.

"I think it's more that it's just not my style." And yet...without Greg, was it going to be tolerable at all? Her phone pinged with a notification.

Greg: Home.

Tharushi: Already?

Greg: Dr. Baker needed me for a shift. Kyle's taking care of Ainsley. She's got the flu.

Clues she hadn't realized she was collecting started adding up in her head...the way Ainsley had come in to see Winnie, and then how she'd avoided the shrimp at the Santiam party, sipping a club soda...then left early.

Tharushi: No, she doesn't.

Greg: No way. You're good, but even you can't diagnose her from two thousand miles away.

Tharushi: Put your money where your mouth is, Backwater.

Greg: Fine. Ten bucks says she's got the flu.

Tharushi: And my ten bucks says she's pregnant.

Sunila was peeking over her shoulder. "Who's that?"
"My roommate."
"Your *roommate?* You live with a *guy?* See, this is why I need to move to the West Coast." Sunila picked up a cute plaid pageboy hat and put it on her head, as if the matter was decided.

    Greg: Did you ever decide whether to talk to Hattie about Mr. Oberst?

    Tharushi: No. Not yet. Still thinking.

    Greg: I really don't think either of them would mind. You know Timberites are nosy as heck.

    Tharushi: Yes, but I'm not a Timberite, am I?

"It's not like that," Tharushi muttered, her cheeks heating. "We're just friends."
"And Auntie Dinithi didn't mind?" Sunila blew out an impressed breath. "My amma would never be that chill."
"Once she got to know him, she liked him. But they weren't wild about the idea at first."
Their mothers approached, effectively ending the conversation, and they went and paid for their purchases. The women paused to bundle back up before they stepped out into the bright sunshine. The city sparkled with white lights and red bows and greenery. They walked by the giant Christmas tree in Millennium Park, and Tharushi smiled at all the people out

ice skating, holding hands so they didn't fall on their backsides. *Greg would do that for me. He has already, in so many ways.*

"Amma," she said quietly, and her mother dropped back, leaning in to hear her. "I've been thinking. Do you think Dr. Kavinda would help me find a new internship?" He was an old family friend, and one of the people who'd gotten her thinking about medicine in the first place.

Dinithi pulled back, surprise written in her wide eyes. "But you only have a year left. Then won't you be leaving anyway?"

Tharushi shrugged, casting her gaze toward the ice skaters again. Her mom stopped walking, and the others noticed. She waved them on ahead, and they waved back as they continued toward the elevated train station.

"What is this about, diyaṇiya? Hmm?" She pushed Tharushi's curls over her shoulder in an affectionate gesture. "You're doing well there. Why not stay?"

"I don't know if I can take it," she whispered. "Living there alone." It was part of the truth; she didn't go to a full confession, not wanting to start an argument in public.

Her mother made a sympathetic sound in the back of her throat and pulled her into a hug, her heavy bags crowding in too. "These things are hard, yes. But you will get through it. You are strong."

"I hate it there, Amma," she said. "It's too far away and it's damp and everything has either moss or mold growing on it. I've held on for two years, yes. But I don't know if it makes sense to stay there now. Not if I could go somewhere where I can finish my cardiac internship as well."

Amma tapped her chin, which Tharushi thought was a bit dramatic. Then again, she was the one considering upending her career over a man whose real affections for her were un-known.

"I will speak to Uncle Mohan if you want me to. But I will say this: do not change pillows to get rid of a headache. Because wherever this new internship is, Greg will not be there, will he?"

Her stomach dropped like she was in a plane that just pitched down. She turned to Amma as they climbed the stairs to the train platform. "You like Greg, right, Amma? Like if..." Tharushi hesitated. "If we were more than roommates, what would you think?"

Amma smiled. "I would think that I want my daughter to be happy. Only that."

"I'm not saying that's how things are," she amended quick-ly. "He's going back to Bluewater, as far as I know."

"The whiteness of the crane, eh?" her mother said, giving her one more squeeze before she linked their arms and pulled her forward. "I'm sorry. But you are strong. I know you will be fine." *The whiteness of the crane appears only when it flies.* It was true; she only realized how much she needed him, how much she wanted him, once she knew he was leaving. *But maybe he's not. Maybe it's not too late. But if that was his plan, why hasn't he told me?* If she texted him to ask now, it would be awkward. But if she was going to make plans...Tharushi sighed. She pulled out her phone as they walked.

Tharushi: when do you leave for Bluewater again?

That was reasonable, right? Wanting to know his plans? It was conceivable that she had another roommate coming in.

Greg: Not sure yet. I think I'm done with work on the 9th.
Tharushi: Okay.
Greg: Having fun with your family?
Tharushi: Of course.

She smiled at her relatives as they climbed the stairs to join them. She would do some calling around tonight herself. There had to be someone out there who wanted a smart, capable Asian doctor on their staff; surely she could find somewhere she'd like better, now that there was no reason to stay. Somewhere far, far away from Timber Falls.

CHAPTER SEVENTEEN

GREG STARED GUILTILY down at his phone, still displaying his texts with Tharushi. Dr. Baker hadn't called him in. He'd come back early to arrange for delivery of his Christmas present to her. But it turned out, getting the piano up the apartment stairs wasn't included. So he'd had to improvise. He squeezed himself past the large instrument to take his place on one of the upper corners.

They'd only moved it about two feet when Daniel cursed loudly. "What is this even made of? Is this the lightest one you could find?"

"Are you sure she doesn't play the violin?" Kyle asked, his breath puffing out in little clouds.

"Come on, guys. We can do this."

"Says the guy on the uphill side of the piano..." Trevor quipped.

"We've got this!" Greg yelled, pumping one fist into the air.

"Don't let go!" the other three bellowed.

"It's no use," Kyle said, his chest heaving. "The steps are too slippery. We'll have to try something else." They carefully let the piano slide back down the ramp, and Greg stabilized it, all the while feeling like his big romantic gesture was slipping away. Turning away from the group, Kyle pulled out his phone and made a call. Daniel shook out his hair and pulled it back, glaring at the piano like it had personally wronged him.

"Do you think more momentum would help?" Trevor asked, rubbing at his smooth chin.

"I don't know, man," Greg said, patting the instrument affectionately. "But we've gotta get it up there somehow. It'll mean so much to her."

Trevor popped an eyebrow. "Did you take the job? So you're finally going to ask her out?"

"I don't know yet on the job. And you say that like it's simple. Oh yes, just ask out the girl you already live with. It won't be awkward *at all* if she says no."

"I mean, I feel like she's going to know how you feel about her when she sees this," Daniel said, gesturing to the piano.

"She might not. Maybe it's a nice Christmas thing one roommate does for another..." Greg let his voice trail off as the other two shook their heads at him. He sighed. "I'm still trying to decide on the ask-out."

"All right," Kyle said, in that authoritative tone that he often used to snap the interns to attention. "I've got more help coming, but they're about half an hour away."

"More help?" Greg asked, perplexed.

"My dad, my sister, and Carter Carpenter."

Greg felt the blood drain out of his face. "You called Carter? He *hates* me, man. I broke up with Martina a while ago...but I'm sure he still hates me."

"Carter doesn't seem like much of a hater to me," Daniel said, cocking his head. "What makes you think—"

"I just know, okay?" He was only panicking a little bit. But his voice sounded like he was panicking a lot. "Whenever he brings his mom into the hospital, he looks at me like I licked all the Christmas cookies."

"No, he looks at you like you licked his *wife*," Trevor offered, and the other men chuckled. Except Greg. There was nothing funny about this.

"I did not! We only made out once and it wasn't even that great. I was thinking about Tharushi the entire time."

"Dude." Daniel's brow was furrowed. "You gotta tell her."

"You guys don't understand; she *hates* it here. Like, *hates* it. More than Winchester hates working Saturdays, more than Klinger hates being in the army. Hates it. And you guys have a Subway. If she hates it here, then moving to Bluewater with me is going to be out of the question."

"How could she hate it here?" Kyle asked, astonished, one hand to his chest like he was personally offended.

"I don't know!" Greg yelled, throwing out his arms. "I think it's great!"

"It's totally great," Daniel agreed, and Trevor just nodded. They chatted for a few more minutes about Tharushi and how wrong she was about their town until Evan and Maggie pulled up. She reminded Greg a lot of his sisters—she seemed very sensible. Carter pulled up a few minutes later.

"Hey everybody," he greeted, and Greg couldn't tell if he was purposely avoiding his gaze. "Is this the piano, I assume?"

Maggie frowned. "We're getting this...up there?"

"Ooh! I brought ropes and gloves. Thought we could rig up a pulley system using the banister at the top..." Evan's idea turned out to be a good one, and Greg and Carter were assigned to be the anchors at the bottom. They got it about halfway up before the guys pushing needed a break. So they were assigned to just...hold.

"So this is for Tharushi?" Carter grunted.

"Yeah." He adjusted his grip on the rope, muscles tight.

"Nice. She played with my mom a few times at the hospital." He wiped his sweaty forehead on his shoulder. "'Heart and Soul' or something."

"She's amazing." It felt weird to admit that to a virtual stranger, but Carter nodded.

"I hope she's worth the hernia I'm getting."

Laughing made it hard to hold on. "She is." Greg craned his neck to see what was happening. "Are you guys almost ready to keep going? We're kind of dying over here."

A chorus of voices answered in the affirmative, and a few difficult minutes later, success was theirs. Greg rushed up the stairs as soon as they could drop the rope and check it out—he'd chosen an upright so it would fit well into the space by the front door. It didn't look any worse for wear, but he still wanted to wipe it down and make sure everything was working right. That would've been a smart thing to do at the bottom of the stairs...but almost anything was fixable, right? He started to worry about why it had been so cheap.

But when Trevor sat down and played a jazzy version of "O Tannenbaum," he knew it would be fine. The rich sound of the strings filled the small room, not quite covering the sound of conversation among friends. He'd met some wonderful people here; how many people would take a morning of their break to push someone else's piano up all these stairs? Greg pulled out his phone and ordered pizza. He couldn't let them leave without thanking them.

"How things change, eh?" Evan joked, elbowing Greg in a friendly way as he pressed in toward the table to grab a slice of meat lovers pizza. "I remember when you two moved in. I wasn't sure you were going to get along."

"Me either," Greg admitted. "But we worked it out."

"You're going to tell her!" Trevor called from across the room. "You're doing that!"

"Oh," Evan said, eyebrows high. "Was this a romantic gesture?"

"Kinda," Greg said, trying to keep from blushing.

"Even better! I love a good love story. Do you have a ring yet?"

Greg choked on his bite of Hawaiian. "Ring? What? No! We're not at the ring stage. I haven't even kissed her yet."

The men started asking overlapping questions with varying levels of confusion.

"Dr. Trout knows what he's doing," Maggie interjected, silencing the men. "He's got this." Privately, she turned to him. "She's gonna love it. Don't worry about it."

"You think?" They had him doubting himself now.

"Definitely. Things for making art are fantastic in every form." She glanced at their still-undecorated Christmas tree. "Do you want some help with that, too, while I'm here?"

"I can't afford twenty dollars an hour," he admitted with a smile, but she waved off his concern.

"You need ambiance if you're going to admit your feelings. This one's on me."

One by one, as they finished their food, his friends helped decorate their tree until it was a tinseled, colored-light, over-baubled monstrosity. Greg loved it. And he thought Tharushi would, too. Everything was ready; now all he had to do was wait. Turned out, that was harder than getting either the tree or the piano up the stairs. He'd had help with that.

There was no way he was sleeping tonight.

CHAPTER EIGHTEEN

THARUSHI HAD BEEN SITTING at baggage claim at PDX for fifteen minutes when Greg came running up.

"I'm sorry, I'm sorry," he panted, going straight for her luggage. "Big accident on I-5. I didn't—" He bent over and put his hands on his knees, trying to catch his breath. "I didn't leave enough time."

"Are you all right?"

"Yeah, just—just give me a minute. I'll be fine." He gestured to her. "How was your flight?"

"Oh, you know."

He shook his head. "Nope. I've never been."

Tharushi blinked at him. "Never been...on an airplane?"

"Never had anywhere I wanted to go."

She'd been on international flights back and forth to Bandaranaike Airport several times before she'd even started elementary school. Tired as she was, she was tempted to march back up to the ticket counter, buy two tickets and take him somewhere just for the heck of it. But he was too practical for that, and he was already headed toward the elevators with most of her luggage.

"It was uneventful," she said when she caught up with him. "Thanks for asking."

Greg smiled at her, and she smiled back as a reflex. They'd only been apart for a few days, and she'd missed him so much. She was not going to survive when he left; there was definitely some self-pity baking in her future. *If he left…*

When they got back to I-5, she turned to him. "So it looks like I might be leaving Timber Falls, too."

"What?" His face had gone frighteningly white, especially considering they were driving sixty-five miles an hour. "What happened?"

"Nothing happened. I just decided I might as well find somewhere that suits me better."

"Oh." He was quiet for longer than she was comfortable with. "I see."

"That would free up the apartment for other interns. The cohort coming in is big. I don't know where she's putting them all."

"I think it would look better on your resume if you finished your general residency first. You don't want them to think you can't stick with something."

She sighed. "I may have to. I haven't had any luck so far in finding something else."

"It's only one more year. You can do it. You already know everyone here, their systems. It's not worth going through that plus the expense and hassle of moving for just one year."

A thought niggled at the back of her mind. "You seem awfully invested in me staying in Oregon."

"No," he said quickly. "I just don't want to see you hurt your career. That's all." At least he was watching the road again. "What did you do in Chicago?"

They caught each other up on how they'd spent their time, but she left out how much time she'd spent staring off into space, wondering if he was going to stay at Santiam. Wondering if there was any way she could convince him without coming clean about how she felt about him. She didn't think so. Disappointing.

She was still thinking about that conversation she'd overheard between Mr. Oberst and those suits, too. What was her responsibility there? She certainly didn't want anyone taking advantage of him, but if he wanted to sell, he had the right to. Still, she wondered if Hattie would want to know about it. It seemed like she could be helpful if Mr. Oberst wanted it.

They were into that corridor of trees now, towering on either side of them. What had felt almost sinister when she arrived now felt strangely comforting. So did being with Greg. When she got out of the truck, the smell of damp pine needles and trees had her shoulders relaxing and a small smile on her face. Chicago was familiar, but it wasn't...home? She didn't know when that had happened. She didn't like small towns. She never had. But somehow, this one had worked its way into her heart more than she'd realized. And like another crane's belly, it had taken leaving to realize it.

She grabbed her carry-on and tromped up the stairs, but the door was locked. Tharushi turned to him, annoyed.

"You *locked* the *door*?"

"Hang on, just—" He was charging up the stairs after her, her big suitcase in hand. "I'm coming."

"I don't even carry a key with me anymore, you've gotten me so used to it being left wide open all the time. You told me the country was safe."

Greg didn't laugh. In fact, he was fumbling with his keys, muttering under his breath, until he finally found the right one. He opened the door for her, and she gave him a skeptical look as she went inside. She reached to drop her bag in its usual place by the door, but there was something in the way. A big something. A big, brown, upright, black-and-white keyed something.

"What did you do?" She covered her mouth. He was shifting his weight like he was nervous; it was clearly his doing. He watched her warily until she let her hands fall away from her face, revealing her expression of awe.

"Merry Christmas, Tharushi."

"How did you..." She looked around, as if she expected more people to be there. "How in the world did you get this up here?"

"I had help," he said, taking off his stocking hat to run a hand through his hair, which was curling on one side and not the other, like he'd fallen asleep with it wet. "Lots of help."

She turned back to the instrument again; she couldn't help it. She touched the keys reverently, barely letting her fingertips rest on them before turning to him with deep emotion in her heart.

"I wasn't sure how it would feel to come back here. It felt so nice to be where I belong, back with my family and friends. We went shopping and we went to Millennium Park to see the Christmas tree. It was snowing, and I had my cousins and my aunties with me, and it was just...perfect." Greg looked like he might throw up, so she hurried on.

"But then I texted you, and I realized I couldn't..." She let her bags drop with a thud. "It's you. You make this bearable. Not just the wonderful things you do," she said, gesturing to the piano, "but the wonderful person you are. You're wonderful. I mean, you're backwater, annoyingly humble and you don't load the dishwasher correctly, but..."

"All right, Peaches, that's enough," he grumbled, and she realized she was smiling so hard, her face actually hurt.

"You're wonderful," she whispered again, and he shuffled forward. She felt drawn to him like a cat to tinsel. She didn't know what he was going to do when he arrived, but she was ready to find out.

"Thank you for coming back," he murmured. "I'm glad you did." Greg tentatively reached out his arms, and she gladly stepped into them.

"Yeah, because you'd be stuck with a piano you can't play..."

"Not just that. But yes, that, too."

"I can't believe you did this for me." She knew she was repeating herself, but she couldn't help it. She was entirely overwhelmed by it.

He kept holding her, but she could hear the relief in his voice. "Well, I couldn't have you unable to process your feelings when I'm gone."

"Are you really leaving?" she whispered. "Someone said..." She bit her lip. Maybe she shouldn't have asked.

"Go on."

"Someone said you'd been offered a job here."

"Yeah."

"So?" She pulled back to see his face. "You turned it down, right? Because of Bluewater?"

"Um." He looked past her to the Christmas tree, and she saw all the tiny lights reflected in his eyes, his skin awash in the gentle light. "Not yet."

"Why?" Her voice came out breathy and weird, but she ignored that.

His gaze came back to her face, and his brown eyes were stormy; she could practically see the hesitation and indecision warring inside him—warring and winning. "Why?" he echoed.

"Yes," she said softly. "Why?" She kept her arms firmly around his waist. He was not getting away this time. First when they said goodbye at the airport, and now this? *Just tell me. Tell me it's for me.*

"I, um..." he stammered. "That is...I just thought maybe..." His gaze bounced between her and the piano, and she thought she knew what he was trying to say. It was time to be brave.

"Greg."

"Hmm?"

"I'd like you to kiss me."

He stared at her, and for one heart-stopping second, she was sure she'd made a huge mistake. Then he leaned in and his warm lips pressed against hers. She pulled him closer, and he seemed to take that as encouragement. His fingertips dug into her hips a little, and her heart did a few backflips as she realized *this was really happening.* Her brain was trying to jump straight to the *what does this mean* phase, but she ignored it.

When his unsure fingers grazed her neck, she ran her tongue curiously along the seam of his lips, and he opened to her with a little groan. All other thoughts fell away as she relaxed into his arms and his kisses, the scent of the Christmas tree next to them competing with his woodsy cologne. She struggled with her coat, not wanting to break their connection for anything, and she heard him do the same as his coat flopped to the floor. Tharushi touched his soft sweater, running her hands over his chest and shoulders.

"This new?"

"Lynne made it." Apparently, that was all the pause he was willing to take to explain because he dove back into their kisses like it was his new favorite thing. *Mine too.* Nestled in his arms with his lips caressing hers, her aching feet were forgotten, her early morning irrelevant. She felt like she could run to Portland and back.

After not long enough, Greg pulled back, resting his forehead against hers, their noses touching tenderly.

"What now?" she asked.

His gaze was hazy and his lips were pinker than usual, and the effect was heady. "Um..." He glanced around. "Are you hungry?"

"You sound like my mother," she said with a laugh. "Here." She tugged him over to the couch. "Talk me through this job situation."

The man unloaded on her like a dump truck. She held his hand and listened, nodding when appropriate. And to her surprise, it didn't feel scary at all. They always talked things through; doing it while holding his hand made it feel safer, if anything. Tharushi didn't feel like she was always the best advisor when it came to emotional problems, but she was willing to try. Whenever she didn't know what to say, her impulse was usually to retreat...but having a physical connection made her feel like she was still supporting him, even though she didn't have answers. And she liked that. When he finished, he curled up and put his head in her lap.

"Wow. Sorry. You don't know how much I wanted to talk to you about this. It was killing me." She let go of his hand and put her fingers in his hair, raking them gently through his light brown waves. When he shuddered, she pulled the quilt off the back of the couch and laid it over him.

"Don't apologize. What do you want to do?" she asked, still playing with his hair. *So soft.*

"I want to do both. I want to stay here with you, especially now that I know that you're...I mean, I assume we're..."

"Yes."

"But I also don't want to disappoint anyone back home. You should've heard my sister June talking about how great it would be when we're all together again..."

"But someone is going to be disappointed no matter what. Whether that's you or me or June. So all you're deciding now is *who* to disappoint."

He was silent for a moment, then he reached up and squeezed her leg. "Well, I know who I don't want to disappoint."

"Yeah. Everyone."

He chuckled. "No, goofball. You." He hesitated. "Are you going to try to transfer to another hospital no matter what?"

"No, I'll stay if you do." She felt that was a bit obvious, but understood that he needed reassurance after all that had gone unsaid between them.

"Because if you really think you should go, you should."

"Look at me."

He turned over, so he was looking up at her.

"I want to be together. I can't promise anything, but I like being with you."

"I like being with you, too." He sat up and leaned in to kiss her, and the sheer sweetness of it made her tingle down to her toes. "Let's go get some dinner. There's no food here."

"You didn't go shopping?"

"In what space? I was busy trying to get that musical monstrosity up the freaking stairs! And you're welcome, by the way."

Tharushi laughed and kissed him again, just because she could. "All right. But I get to pick."

"As long as I get to pay."

She'd never taken off her shoes when they got home, so she just put her coat back on. "You never paid for my dinner before..."

He cocked his head, as if considering this. "Yes, but this is kind of our first date." Well, that rankled a bit. It wasn't like she needed long-winded professions of love or anything, but...

"No, it's not."

"It's not?" He grinned. "Do I have to ask you out properly? Get down on one knee or something?"

"Yes," she said simply as she breezed by him, making sure to grab her wallet on the way, then headed down the stairs. The deer who liked to eat Mr. Wilson's roses was back.

"Shoo!" she yelled, waving an arm at him, and the creature stared at her for a moment before it went back to eating. She kicked a rock in its direction, not hard enough to reach it, and then it scampered off. When she slammed the passenger side door to the truck, her phone buzzed.

Greg: I've been thinking about this a lot, and I'd love to take you somewhere special. Would you be available tomorrow night for a date?

Tharushi: I'll have to check my schedule.

She could hear his answering laughter through the windshield as he approached the truck, and she grinned at him. This was going to be good.

CHAPTER NINETEEN

GREG DECIDED HE WASN'T going to try to kiss her again; he didn't want to push his luck. This all felt too good to be true. He spent their whole dinner just grinning at her like a goof, teasing her about the hot sauce running down her arms and how she'd ordered a quesadilla as big as her face. Their family stories were remarkably similar—there were some things about coming from a four-kid family that spanned culture.

He'd wanted Thai, but she was still a bit leery of Asian food after his sesame incident at Kyle's. He knew it had messed her up a bit—roommates don't usually sleep on each other's floors, after all—but he hadn't realized her insecurity would last this long. He was not surprised when she decided to go for a run, though he felt he could barely walk with how much he'd eaten.

"Which direction?" he asked out of habit.

"North," she said, rolling her eyes. "Always north." When she pulled him in by his sweater to give him a long kiss goodbye, he nearly melted at her feet. It had been an emotional day...when she'd started talking about leaving Timber Falls, he'd panicked a little. If she left, all of this would've been for naught. But then she'd loved the piano, and she'd asked him to kiss her, and he did...and then spilled the beans about the job offer.

She'd confirmed the date over dinner, and he knew he'd need to pull out all the stops on this one. If it went well...no, one thing at a time. That was too much pressure to put on one interaction. But he was ninety percent sure he was going to stay in Santiam. She'd been the biggest factor, and apparently, she was into him. He still couldn't quite believe it.

He went to bed early to read, but he left his door open a crack so he could hear her come in. When she needed to unplug, she ran. When he needed to unplug, he read. Getting lost in fantastic worlds of swords and sorcery was his favorite. He was just at the part where the main character was getting a magic metal arm, so engrossed in the thick book that he jumped at the sound of her voice.

"I'm home."

He smiled from where he lay on his side, one arm tucked under his head. "Good run?"

She nodded. "And I closed the barn door myself."

His grin broadened. "So now that we're dating, I'm not allowed to take care of you?"

She scowled. "You're all cozy in bed. I was already wet." She was hovering at the doorway, he noticed. The boundaries were getting a bit blurred. Normally, they never came into each other's space without an express invitation. And for now, maybe that was still a good idea. "Also, this was in the mailbox." She held up a white envelope. "I think it's a Christmas card from Mrs. Foster."

"Nice. Stick it on the table for me?"

"Sure. Sweet dreams." That was assured. All he had to do was play back the events of today.

"You too."

THE NEXT MORNING, HE was munching on his corn-flakes when he opened the Christmas card, and his jaw went slack. Tharushi came out, dressed for work in gray suit pants and a white blouse. He rushed over to her, holding out the open card.

"What do you see here?"

She scanned the card calmly. "A somewhat-clichéd Christmas card?"

"No," he said, shaking the paper insistently. "Look with your doctor eyes."

She took it from him, scrutinizing it closer. "Micrographia."

"Right? Look how tiny her handwriting is. I can't believe I didn't see it earlier. Come on, we've got to get to work."

Tharushi lifted an eyebrow. "I hate to point this out, but you're the one still in your pajamas, not me."

"Right. Yes. Let me just…" Greg darted back into his room and kicked the door shut. He was dressed in two minutes flat, and he didn't look anywhere as classy as Tharushi, but he never did, so that was fine. She was waiting in the truck for him, scrolling through her phone and drinking her coffee, and he got to the hospital in record time.

"Dr. Baker?" She pivoted from her conversation with Daniel and one of the new interns. "Could you consult on a case for me?" In his haste, he'd forgotten to bring the card, but no matter. She followed him down the hall toward Anne's room.

"What's up?"

"I have a hunch about Mrs. Foster's condition…"

"I'm all ears," Dr. Baker said.

"She sent me a Christmas card, and Dr. Udawatte and I both noticed that her handwriting was tiny."

"Micrographia? Are you thinking Parkinson's?"

He nodded. "Given her recent fall and constipation, it's the strongest possibility right now." They reached her doorway, and Dr. Baker gestured for him to go first.

"Good morning, Mrs. Foster. How was your holiday?"

"Just fine," she said quietly, pushing herself up in bed, and he moved to prop another pillow behind her back.

"I wanted to thank you for your Christmas card. Did you write it yourself?"

She turned her head to give him a side-eyed glare. "Yes…"

He nodded. "I thought so. Mrs. Foster, we think you might have Parkinson's. We'll run more tests to be sure, but it's a strong possibility." He'd learned to stop talking after he delivered a potential diagnosis; patients often stopped listening for a few seconds as they processed.

"Oh."

As he'd expected, her face showed little response. She wore the same serious look she usually had.

"Facial masking," Dr. Baker murmured, and Greg watched Mrs. Foster carefully. That was consistent with Parkinson's, too. He didn't know why he hadn't noticed it before. Then, turning to Mrs. Foster, Dr. Baker said at a normal volume, "I'd like to refer you to Dr. Rose, our neurologist here at Santiam. Parkinson's can be tricky to diagnose. I'm sorry it took so long, but the good news is that you can go home today and come back for your appointment with Dr. Rose."

"I'll call Hattie," she said, reaching for her phone.

"Stay here in case Hattie wants to talk to you," Dr. Baker said to him. "I have another appointment, but please come find me later."

Greg nodded, but inside, he thought he might wait until after his date with Tharushi tonight. He'd know more then.

CHAPTER TWENTY

THARUSHI HELD A CURVED surgical needle above the young man's arm, poised to start. The suture was attached to the end, the patient was relatively calm, and based on her poking, his arm was numb. Privately, she thought his brain might also be slightly numb, given that he cut himself open trying to do tricks with a butterfly knife. She could hear Dr. Devereaux clear his throat behind her. It was nice to have him back.

"May I ask what you're waiting for?" His light Southern accent made everything sound so polite.

"Just...confidence," she said with a sigh, and Dr. Devereaux chuckled. "Do you not remember what happened with the banana peel?" He'd been the extra help Dr. Baker had conscripted, and his first assignment had been to suture a banana peel. It had gone better than the pig's foot, but by the time she'd gotten it acceptable, it had been black and leathery.

"I do. But you've come a long way since then."

Now her patient, Ryder Zane, did look a little bit nervous. He adjusted his trucker hat. "Maybe he should do it."

"Now, just give her a minute. Dr. Udawatte is fully capable of stitching you up, Mr. Zane. I wouldn't put you in her hands if I didn't think she could do it."

151

Tharushi pushed her shoulders back. "If you don't want to see when the needle goes in, you should look away now." Ryder's dad was next to him, and he put a hand on his son's shoulder. When Ryder did look away, Tharushi got started. It was a fairly straight incision, so it didn't take long. She didn't know why she'd been so nervous. It was one of her weaker points, but as a cardiologist, she'd never have to perform surgery. Still, it was worth knowing how to do, and she was getting better.

She went over the discharge information with her patient and his father, emphasizing to keep the stitches clean but dry. As they left, she checked her phone: 7:45. Greg would be waiting around for her somewhere. She shot off a text.

> **Tharushi:** Ready to go home? Just need to change.
> **Greg:** Yup.

Once she was back in her regular clothes, she pulled down her hair and fluffed it out. Hopefully he wouldn't mind end-of-day curls that were a bit low on bounce. They'd both worked a full shift, after all. She grabbed her backpack and strode through the hall, keeping an eye out for him. When she'd made a full circle around the floor without finding him, Tharushi stopped by reception.

"Have you seen Dr. Trout?" Why was Nurse Franklin looking at her like that? Amanda knew they commuted together. There was nothing strange about the question. Amanda jerked her head toward the front doors, and Tharushi turned to look. No wonder she hadn't recognized him—he was wearing a charcoal grey suit and holding a dozen red roses. Was that...yes, he was wearing a vest. She was weak for vests. Tharushi felt a slow smile spread across her face.

"Have fun," Amanda whispered.

"I plan to," Tharushi replied, but her eyes were still on Greg. She crossed the lobby quickly and gave him a peck on the cheek. "Hi."

"Hi." He had a big silly grin on his face, and based on the strength of his cologne, he'd gone home to shower and change. "These are for you."

"I kind of figured. They're beautiful."

"No, these are average. *You're* beautiful." He offered her his arm, and she took it as she sniffed the delicate blooms. They must have set him back a pretty penny. He led them through the sliding front doors and out into the parking lot.

"Where are we headed?"

He opened the truck door for her. "I made reservations at Bianchi's. Italian. No Asian food, because I know you're still nervous about the sesame thing." She was. She knew it was pointless; he was careful. But she couldn't get over it. Hopefully soon, she'd be able to relax about it, when the event wasn't so fresh in her mind.

"Sounds good." Bianchi's was in Salem, so he got on the highway going away from Timber Falls. He told her about his day—Dr. Baker agreed with his diagnosis for Anne Foster, and they'd been able to send her home. She told him about her day, too, and the surgery. Really, it was their normal end-of-day debrief...and yet, it wasn't. That much was obvious when he went around to open her door for her again.

They were seated right away, and he ordered a bottle of chardonnay for them.

"I won't have much. Is that okay?"

"Sure," she said, tucking her wallet under her leg in the booth. Silence enveloped them; the couples and groups around them were talking, laughing. But for once, she didn't know what to say to him. Her brain was fried from her shift, and he'd gone to all this trouble...

"You okay?" he asked softly, and she snapped out of it.

"Yes. Of course." She forced a smile, but the slight tilt of his head told her he knew her better than that. That was the problem with dating someone who already knew you very well—she was not going to be able to fake her way through this date.

"Did something happen today?"

"No, I just..."

"Hi, I'm Maxim, and I'll be your waiter tonight." Tharushi thought he looked familiar, but she couldn't place him. She ordered the lasagna, which sounded good and wouldn't be as messy as a pasta dish that might flip red sauce all over her white blouse. Greg ordered a salad, and she frowned at him. This man loved a cheeseburger like nothing else. Why were they here? And why was he ordering the cheapest thing on the menu? They handed over their menus, and as soon as their waiter disappeared into the back, Tharushi slid out of the booth and stood up. She held out her hand. Greg stared at her uncertainly for a minute, then glancing around, he took his napkin off his lap and followed her. Holding his hand, she weaved through the restaurant until she found the long hallway that contained the bathrooms and an area for coats. She dragged him past both, toward a glowing red exit sign, then stopped just before they went outside. They stood there, so close to the exit, she could feel the cold air seeping into the old brick building.

"What is going on?" she hissed. "What are you doing?"

"What do you mean?" he whispered back. "I'm on a date. With you. This is me, on a date."

She folded her arms over her belly. "This wasn't what I wanted."

"It's not?" He seemed so genuinely confused, she almost laughed.

"No," she whispered. "I mean, I wanted time with you. Special time. But I don't need you spending money you don't have on me."

Even in the glow of the exit sign, she could tell he was blushing. "I *have* money—"

"Gregory, you ordered a salad. Are you seriously going to tell me that's what you wanted?"

He glanced down the wood-paneled hallway, then down at his shiny shoes. "No."

"So? What's going on?"

"I was just trying to spoil you a little," he said, his hands coming up to her arms, rubbing them gently. "That's all. I wanted you to know that I get that this is different from how we usually hang out. I wanted you to feel special."

"Greg, you drive me everywhere. You could've made me go get my own car, but you didn't, because you're such a ridiculously nice guy. You bake cookies with me. You go out into the dark to close the scary barn door for me. You let me pilfer your mom's preserves. You share your heart and your thoughts with me. And you bought me a freaking piano." She shuffled closer until she could nestle her head between his neck and his shoulder. "So what I'm trying to say is that I've felt special since the moment we met. I just love being with you, and what I love about it is that there's no pretense, that I can just be myself with you. This is all very sweet, but...it doesn't feel like us."

He bent his head to kiss her. "It doesn't, does it?"

She shook her head, then kissed him again, needing the reassurance and closeness. Also, it felt delightfully taboo to be hiding in the back of the restaurant, making out with her roommate.

"Come on." He took her hand and now it was her turn to be led through the restaurant. Greg wove between the candlelit tables until he found their waiter. "Could we get our food to go?"

The dark-haired man blinked at them. "Certainly, sir." They didn't even go back to their table; Greg reclaimed their coats and they stood close together in the lobby while Maxim brought them their food. Tharushi tried to get Greg to split it with her, but he wouldn't hear of it. *Whatever, I'll get the next one. He's stubborn, but he's no match for me.* He still opened her door when they got back to the truck. He turned on some classic rock, his favorite kind of music, and she sat back in her seat, the hot food bagged up on her lap, as he got back on the highway. But when he blasted right by their driveway, she turned to him.

"Where are we going?"

His grin was lascivious. "There's an aspect of small-town life you haven't experienced yet."

"Oh? I hope it's not being left in the woods."

Greg chuckled. "No, it's better than that."

"Good, because then I'd need all the crap I got you for Christmas, and I don't have it."

He sat up straighter. "You got me a present?" She felt bad she hadn't given it to him yet, so she figured this was a good way to make amends. She'd been too distracted by his present when she got home, even though she'd bought it before their break.

Tharushi sniffed. "I did not get you *a* present. I got you every safety measure for hiking that is buyable." She ticked off on her fingers. "Trekking poles, wool socks, GPS, water filtration straw..."

"You were afraid I was going to get lost or hurt in the woods, weren't you?" He was totally laughing at her. "Tharushi, I rarely go more than two miles from the house."

"How should I know what you do out there?" she said, exasperated. "I just didn't want you going missing in the wilderness of Mount Chewelah when you moved home."

"That's very sweet."

"Oh, hush."

He reached out and put a hand on her leg. "Seriously. You're very thoughtful and considerate, and I appreciate that. I appreciate you." He couldn't really look at her, because he was driving, and she was secretly thankful for his inattention and the dark to hide her hot cheeks.

"Well, I thought I went overboard until I saw yours. Now I'm not sure if I got enough..."

"It wasn't that much. I'm sure you did fine." He gave her leg a tender squeeze. Then he turned his truck off the highway and up onto a forest service access road.

"Seriously, where are we going?"

"Remember Mrs. Foster?"

Tharushi nodded.

"Well, her family used to own a lot of this land north of the highway. They've lived in Timber Falls since way back before the mill went in. So now it's called Foster's Point, and it's become kind of a..." Their headlights swept over several parked cars. "Make-out spot."

"Aren't we too old for this?" she asked, peering nervously at the Honda Civics and Toyota Tercels parked around them.

"I'm not," he said with a grin, taking off his seat belt. "Come on." Was he going to make her eat outside? It was too cold for that. What was he...oh yes, he was coming around to open her door. Great. She slid out, food in hand lest he forget that she was still hungry. But to her surprise, he opened the back door of the truck and motioned her inside.

"Oh thank goodness, I thought you were going to make me eat outside."

"No!" He laughed. "I just can't snuggle with you properly in the front seat. Scoot over." He climbed in after her, and true to his word, he slid right up next to her, their arms and knees touching. "Pass me mine."

"We're going to share," she said, passing him a fork.

"Mmm, romantic," he teased. "Are you going to feed me, too?"

"Keep dreaming," she deadpanned as she opened the lid of the compostable container.

"What if I wanted my salad all to myself?" he asked, nevertheless stabbing himself a large bite of the lasagna.

"Impossible. I know you too well." She took a bite, and the freshness of the sauce landed a bright taste on her tongue. "Mmm. This is really good, though."

"I told you, I wanted you to feel special. You think I didn't do any research?" He took off his jacket and hung it on the hook above the window. He stabbed at the salad, too. "Mmm, salami. I do like salami."

"And banana peppers."

"Yeah, I love banana peppers." He smiled at her. "We're bad at first dates. I'm supposed to be telling you about myself or something."

"Maybe you should quiz me about you instead." Just to be fair, she took a bite of the salad, too. But then she noticed the waiter had tucked in some garlic bread for them...

"What's my favorite piece of clothing?"

"Your Bluewater Buccaneers sweatshirt. What's mine?"

"Your running jacket."

"Correct. It has built-in reflective panels. And it's so comfortable." She took a bite of her garlic bread—the butter had melted into the tiny crevices. "What's my favorite book?"

"*Outliers* by Malcolm...what's his name."

"No point," she said, waving her bread at him. "You have to get the author, too."

"Um..." He was gently tapping his fist against his forehead. "Malcolm...Malcolm...Goodwell?"

"Gladwell. Close enough. And I know you don't have one."

"That's right because, unlike some people, I am an equal opportunity book reader. Though I'm really enjoying this fantasy I'm reading right now. Hey, there's garlic bread? Were you going to share or hog it all yourself?"

"Hog it all," she said with a grin.

"Greedy," he chided, then he leaned forward and kissed her, the salty taste of the salami still on his lips. It was just a quick one, but the desire for more was in his gaze when he sat back. She hastily wiped her hands on a napkin, then reached out and put her hands on both sides of his face, pulling him toward her again.

"I'm not greedy," she said against his lips. "I just know what I want."

Without breaking their tender staring contest, Greg started closing containers and setting them on the console between the front seats.

"Is dinner over?" Tharushi asked, her voice low, and Greg swallowed hard, then nodded. Once their laps were clear, he pulled her over onto his, sitting sideways, and she smiled as she kissed him again. Before long, their somewhat foggy windows were completely clouded over.

"Does this feel like us?" he asked, a bit breathless.

She nodded, stealing another kiss. "Just out of curiosity, does Bluewater have a make-out spot?"

"Of course."

A knock on the window made both of them jump, and she scrambled off Greg's lap, but there was no time to do anything else before he rolled down the window. Lizzie Painter stood there in her tan uniform, giant flashlight in hand.

"Evening, Deputy," Greg said, and Tharushi could hear the embarrassment in his voice. *If only he knew how much lipstick was on his face.*

"Hi Dr. Trout..." Lizzie squinted into the darkness of the car, but Tharushi knew she'd be harder to see. "Dr. Udawatte."

"Do we need to move along?"

"No, you two are fine. I only have to tell the teenagers to move along," she said with a smile. "Sorry to interrupt. Enjoy your evening." They were closest to the road, and Tharushi could hear other cars starting all around them. Soon they'd have the place to themselves.

"Thank you, Deputy. You have a nice evening, too," Greg called as she headed back to her cruiser. Then he cranked the window up and covered his face with both hands.

"Are you embarrassed?" she teased, pulling at his wrists. "This was your idea, what did you think was going to happen?"

He was laughing, his face bright pink, when he let them drop. "I don't know. I just thought it'd be fun."

"It *was* fun," she said, kissing him again. They kissed until they both got too cold to keep going, then they went home. As he pulled into the driveway, she realized she didn't know exactly how to end this date—or how he was expecting to end it—and that set her stomach buzzing with nervous energy. She got her door open before he could come around, but on their way up the stairs, he grabbed her hand. He didn't let go as he opened the front door, even though he let her enter first. But he did pull her over to her bedroom door, then paused. The nerves that had been crawling around in her stomach shot up into her throat. He gently turned her until she was standing inside the doorway, and he was leaning on the jamb, as if this were her front door.

"I had a great time tonight," he said, taking both her hands and gazing into her eyes. "When can I see you again?"

Oh, is that how we're going to play this, Greg? I can handle that.

"Breakfast not soon enough?"

He ignored her joke. "How's Wednesday?"

"Trying to nail down the second date at the door, not by phone later? Bold, Dr. Trout."

"Yeah, well," he said, tugging her a little closer, "when I connect with someone, I want to spend as much time with them as I can." He rubbed the back of her hand with his thumb, looking down at their joined hands.

"Yeah," she murmured, "I think I know how that feels. Wednesday works for me."

"Good. I'll see you then," he said, letting go and stepping back. "Good night, Tharushi."

"Good night." She would've closed her door anyway to change out of her work clothes, but it felt silly to do it to mark the end of their date. Still, she pushed it shut, glad he seemed to understand that she needed a moment to think and have a little space to herself. Tharushi wandered around her room, putting things away, but it didn't take long enough. She bounced on her toes, looking out the front window. It was too late to go running, but she had too much energy to go to sleep. Tharushi pulled back her hair and changed into yoga clothes, determined to try to settle down. But she just couldn't focus on the woman's calm instructions. She slapped her laptop shut and stared at her closed door. It had never bothered her before. But right now, it did.

She crossed the room and opened it. Greg was in his traditional spot on the couch, wearing jeans and a T-shirt now, bare feet up on the coffee table. His computer was on his lap and he had *M*A*S*H* on the TV and it was like getting a big hug; she needed that familiarity right now.

"Hey," he said, glancing up at her. "How was your date?"

"Pretty good," she said, crossing the room to sit next to him, mirroring his relaxed posture. "He bought me flowers and expensive Italian food and then we made out in his truck."

His eyes widened comically. "You made out with him on the first date? You'd better be careful. Don't want him to get the wrong idea."

"I think it was the right idea," she said, tilting her head until it rested on his shoulder. "How was yours?"

"Fantastic. I can't wait to do it again."

"Does she know you're leaving?" The vulnerability of her question must have been obvious, because he put aside his computer and took her hand.

"She knows it's a possibility," he said softly. "But I hope she's not worried about it."

"She's trying not to be." She squeezed his hand, and he squeezed back. Then he turned and kissed her forehead with such tenderness, it nearly brought tears to her eyes. She snuggled in harder, watching with him until the episode ended. Then she extricated herself, gave him one more kiss, and went to bed.

CHAPTER
TWENTY-ONE

GREG WALKED BACK INTO Santiam the next morning on a mission. Naturally, he was accosted immediately by Daniel, who needed a second opinion on a baby with a high fever. And then by Amanda, who wanted his signature on some paperwork he'd neglected. And then by Dr. Rose, who wanted his thoughts on Anne's diagnosis. And by the time he finished his rounds and found Dr. Baker, it was lunchtime, and she was eating in the cafeteria with Tharushi, as she often did. Frustrated, he went back to their classroom to eat.

But Kyle was already there. He often ate in there since he found the cafeteria overstimulating, one of the hazards of being autistic.

"May I join you?" Greg asked, and Kyle looked up from his phone and nodded. "How's Ainsley feeling?"

"Pregnant."

"Really?" Greg paused mid-sit. Tharushi had been right. That was annoying. "That's great, man." He refrained from slapping Kyle on the back, since he had been clear that he didn't want unnecessary physical contact. Daniel ignored his rule frequently, but Greg felt uncomfortable doing so. Brothers got a special pass sometimes.

"Yes." Kyle seemed subdued. "It is great."

"You don't seem too excited," Greg commented. *Shoot, was that rude?* He was so distracted by his decision, he wasn't thinking straight. Maybe he shouldn't be talking.

"No, I am. I hadn't planned on having children for several more years, but it appears our contraceptive method has failed." He snapped off a baby carrot with his teeth. "Now I'm just thinking about all the ways my life is going to change. It's a lot."

"I bet."

"I mean, I've already compromised a lot, just having Ainsley in my life. It's a big sacrifice, being in a relationship. And now I'm going to be in a relationship with another person who'll need me even more."

"It'll be worth it, though. Don't you think?"

Kyle munched his sandwich thoughtfully. "I would think so. When I thought Ainsley was engaged to someone else, I felt so sad. Living with her can be complicated, but she's wonderful. I'm sure I'll feel the same way when I see my baby, too." He snapped off another baby carrot. "My *baby*. That's going to take some adjustment."

"Life feels like one adjustment after another sometimes," Greg mused.

"Agreed. But I'm determined to make room for his new person. I mean, I'm the only dad they've got."

Greg thought as they sat in silence, both eating. Kyle was right. Life was always throwing you curveballs—if he could smash one out of the park, shouldn't he try? He hadn't planned on falling in love and wanting to stay here, but that didn't mean he couldn't try to make it work. Bluewater would still be there, and other people could help. Tharushi, however, might move on; she was once-in-a-lifetime, as far as he was concerned.

"Thanks for the talk, Kyle."

"You're welcome," he answered absently, having gone back to reading on his phone. Greg strode down the hallway with such purpose, people got out of his way without him even having to ask. He charged his way into the cafeteria, determined to talk to his boss before he could change his mind.

"Dr. Baker."

She and Tharushi both looked up when he stopped next to their table, a little out of breath.

"I'll take that job…" They both brightened immediately, but he held up a hand. "For one year. And then I reserve the right to reassess my situation."

Dr. Baker bobbed her head. "That sounds fair. I'll draw up the paperwork right now. I'm delighted you'll be continuing with us." She cast Tharushi a meaningful look, then gathered up her lunch debris and left. Tharushi looked like she was going to vibrate out of her chair, and he opened his arms just in time for her to spring into them. He held her close, then whispered in her ear, "What are you doing New Year's Eve?"

When she laughed, it came out thick and watery, and he drew back, concerned. She quickly wiped away the tears, grinning at him. "I'm so glad you're staying. I hated closing that barn door by myself."

"Come here," he said, pulling her into a kiss, not caring at all that they were surrounded by coworkers and patients. He was making the right decision; just looking at her face confirmed it. It wasn't going to be easy, but he was going to take a swing at this curveball—and maybe even get a home run.

CHAPTER TWENTY-TWO

THARUSHI HAD COME STRAIGHT from work for both their dates, so today, she was going all out. Wednesday, Greg had been happy to just take her out on their way home, and they'd laughed over burgers and fries at Annie's in the corner like two loons. But tonight was New Year's Eve, and fast food was not on the menu. She fully intended to knock his socks off. Bold, gold eyeshadow, shiny nude lip color, the rest kept simple...she was still putting on her mascara when Greg knocked.

"Hey in there," he called through the door. "Just wondered if you'll be ready sometime this year."

"Knock off the New Year's Eve jokes," she called back. "You think you're funny, but you're not."

There was silence for a full minute before he cleared his throat. "Why do geese fly south on New Year's Eve?"

"You Googled more jokes, didn't you."

"It's too far to walk. What did the farmer give his wife on New Year's Eve?"

She put on her huge hoop earrings and gave herself a final once-over. "A headache?"

"Hogs and kisses. C'mon, Peaches, you're not even trying. What did the cat say on New Year's Eve?"

Tharushi crossed to the door and opened it. "Meow?"

Greg stared at her, the phone still in his hand, but clearly forgotten. His lips parted a little, and the way his gaze wandered over her from head to toe made her grin.

"I-you-what-" Greg babbled, then put one hand over his mouth like he didn't trust it anymore.

"Thank you, you look nice, too, and also, I'm still waiting for the punchline of that joke."

"Meow," he murmured, his eyes still eating her up. "It was meow. You got it. Wow..." He stepped into her space and put one hand to her cheek, sending sparks to her belly. "Tharushi, you are so beautiful. I mean, you are every day, but tonight...Wow. I don't...I can't even..."

She enjoyed seeing him a bit flustered, but also didn't mind rescuing him once in a while. She tipped her head back and tapped her lips to show him where she wanted her kiss. He gave her one gently.

"Don't want to mess you up before everyone gets to take you in..." he murmured against her lips.

"Is that a promise to mess me up later?" she asked, and he grinned.

"Let's go." He offered her his arm, and she took it, slinging her tiny purse over the other shoulder.

THARUSHI HAD TO GIVE them credit: for a small-town affair, this was classy. There were shrimp cocktails, live music, even an ice sculpture. Had this place been holding out on her all this time? She grabbed a glass of champagne, then hesitated. Greg was a few feet away, talking to Hattie while eating more bruschetta. She waved until she got his attention, then pointed to her glass. He gave her a thumbs-up.

"I just have to tell you, you look amazing." Tharushi turned to find Ainsley at her elbow, a glass of sparkling cider in her hand.

"Oh, thank you. So do you," she returned politely.

"Well, that's a miracle," Ainsley said with a chuckle, "because I am exhausted half the time and throwing up the other half."

"Kyle told us the good news—congratulations!"

Ainsley smiled. "Oh, thank you. Yes, I figured there were no secrets in this town."

Tharushi thought back to what she'd overheard on her run. Leaving Timber Falls even temporarily had been an interesting experience...if she was staying here, if she was making a home here with Greg, then she should act like a Timberite. She wanted to.

She spun her glass nervously. "If someone did know a secret..."

Ainsley cocked her head. "You?"

She nodded. "I overheard something, and I think someone might be in some financial trouble. And the way he's going about solving it might not be good for any of us. Well, maybe for me, but I can drive to Salem for rice noodles."

Ainsley blinked. "You lost me."

Tharushi told her the whole story about her fall and the suits and Mr. Oberst and what she'd heard. Ainsley nodded along, bending closer to hear the story better. When she finished, Ainsley straightened.

"I think you should tell Hattie. She's known him for a long time."

"I just didn't want to betray his trust. Surely he knows he can reach out and ask for help if he needs it."

Ainsley shrugged. "Money stuff is hard. Maybe he's embarrassed. I know life's been hard for him since Bonnie died. It's important to have a partner, isn't it?"

"Oh," Tharushi deadpanned, "that's a smooth segue."

"It is, isn't it? I do my best." Ainsley grinned. "So how long have you two been together?"

"Only a couple of days..." She couldn't help but cast a glance in Greg's direction; he was wearing that suit again. She was a big fan of that suit. "But it's been a long time coming."

"I thought maybe. Who cracked first? Kyle and I may have had a bet going..."

You're wonderful.

"I guess I did. Huh." She turned back to Ainsley. "So who won?"

"He did," Ainsley fumed, and Tharushi laughed. "For someone who can't tell when I'm being sarcastic, he can be pretty perceptive when he wants to be."

"Is he excited to be a dad?"

She grinned. "Oh yeah. After extensive research that I was forced to participate in, he went out and got a crib today. I'm sure he'll have the nursery all set up by Valentine's Day."

"And when are you due?"

"Not until August." Ainsley put a hand to her stomach, but instead of glowing, she looked a little green again. "Hold this for me, will you?"

Tharushi accepted her drink and watched with sympathy as she took off for the bathroom again.

"Hey. Double fisting it?" Greg teased.

"This is Ainsley's. She had to use the restroom. Also, where's my money?"

"Five? Is that what we said?" he asked, getting out his wallet.

"It was ten, and you know it. I should make you give me twenty just for trying to weasel out of it."

"I can't believe you called it from another state. Especially since I was *lying*."

"Serves you right." She was smiling again. It just kept happening, ever since her piano arrived. Ever since she'd finally had the courage to say how she really felt. She wished she'd done it a long time ago, but that was life—there was no going back. "Will you dance with me?"

"Of course." They dropped the drinks off with Kyle, who was arguing with Daniel about the safety of strollers that allowed you to drop the car seat directly into them. It was a slow song, heavy on the saxophone, and she sighed as Greg collected her into his arms. There were a lot of people she cared about in this funny little town tucked against the Cascades. It was something she couldn't imagine when she'd arrived here two years ago, but she couldn't help but feel glad that she'd stuck it out. That they'd gotten through it together.

"So when do you start work?"

His hand was warm on her lower back. "She gave me a little time off, actually. I need to go home and explain to my family in person."

"That makes sense."

He lowered his lips to her ear. "Would you like to come with me?"

That darn smile again—her cheek muscles hurt. "I would love to."

The people around them started counting down to midnight, but she couldn't wait that long. Tharushi grabbed his face and pulled Greg into a kiss, the pretense of dancing forgotten, ringing in the new year with the love of her life.

EPILOGUE

ONE YEAR LATER

"And the award for the most improved in surgery goes to...Tharushi Udawatte!" Dr. Baker announced.

Greg crowed his approval, clapping loudly. "That's my fiancé! Way to go, Peaches!" She waved at him—more of a *stop embarrassing me* than a *hello*—but he just waved back, grinning. He stood in the back of the VA Hall with Daniel and Kyle, who was rocking back and forth incessantly. That wasn't abnormal for Kyle, but in this case, there were special circumstances.

"Do you want me to take one?" Daniel asked.

"No, I've got them," Kyle said quietly, shooting Greg a dirty look as he put a hand on his oldest son's head. Lucas seemed to be the easier of the two; Levi was the fussy one. But at the moment, they were both asleep, strapped to his chest in matching slings.

"Dr. Udawatte has been a real joy to work with. She was part of the first class of interns who came to Santiam, and I have always been grateful for the faith she placed in me. Her diagnostic ability is uncannily accurate, and she is a skilled and dedicated physician who will be very missed." Polite applause rippled through the attendees, and Dr. Baker leaned into the microphone again. "Also, we thank her for giving Dr. Trout a reason to stick around."

Lots of Timberites turned around to smile at him, and he smiled back, even as the pain tugged at his heart. Texas just wasn't going to be the same; it was a great opportunity for Tharushi, and he'd be happy to keep working alongside her, but this little town would be missed by both of them as well. There was still no VolumeMart; Hattie had gone up to Mr. Oberst's place and they'd found a better solution. It was now a premier destination for people looking to play paintball in the woods, and he was tickled to have people coming around. Anne's Parkinson's had progressed somewhat, but she was doing well and planning to go along with the Mind Readers to California next month.

But there were still a lot of things they'd miss: seeing Liam and Levi grow up, as well as Daniel and Winnie's daughter, Kendall. Dr. Baker was finally marrying her long-time boyfriend, Dr. Sokolov. And this new class of interns showed a lot of promise; he was sorry they wouldn't get to watch them change and grow. But Texas would hold new adventures for them, and most importantly, they'd be together. Tharushi strode down the center aisle, and Greg felt a slow smile cross his face.

"Please don't rile Tharushi up," Kyle murmured. "If she wakes the boys, I'll have to go outside. I don't want to have to go outside, it's cold out there."

"It'll be fine," Greg assured him as Tharushi delivered a stinging whack to his arm. "Ow."

"What did I say about the hooting and hollering?" she hissed.

"That you wish I'd do it more often?"

"Try again." She pasted a smile on her face as her parents approached. They were all going out to dinner after this, and then tomorrow, it would be time to finish packing and hit the road.

"Love you, Peaches," he whispered, and she turned and gave him a smile—a real one this time.

"I love you, too. Thank you for staying and seeing me through this last year."

"Thank you for telling me how you really felt. Best present I ever got."

She leaned in, careful not to jostle Kyle and the babies, and gave Greg a kiss. "Me too. And I can't believe I'm saying this, but if Timber Falls led me to you, I guess it's not too bad."

Greg squeezed her tight. "I'm glad you finally came around."

Would you leave a
review?

THE BEST PRESENT YOU could give me this holiday season is the gift of an honest review—small businesses like mine live or die by them! Your review lets others know if they'd enjoy Greg and Tharushi's story and helps give my work credibility in a huge sea of options. Thank you in advance if you're able to help!

Don't miss your
Timber Falls bonus
library!

NEWSLETTERS SUBSCRIBERS have access to six short stories starring your favorite Timberites! Not a newsletter subscriber yet? What are you waiting for? Find a screen and go to http://www.subscribepage.com/timberfalls and sign up now to get sneak peeks at future books, sales and giveaways.

Don't miss a moment of Timber Falls fun!

Could Be Something Good (Daniel and Winnie)
Must be a Mistake (Kyle and Ainsley)
Right Back Where We Started (Martina and Carter)
More Than We Bargained For (Starla and Sawyer)
Just Getting Started (Lizzie and Chase)
No Time Like the Present (Greg and Tharushi)
Don't Push Your Luck (Christopher and Paige)

Also by Fiona West

Rocky Royal Romance (sweet fantasy romance)
Chasing Down Her Highness: a chronically-ill princess who fled from her responsibilities is forced to face the fiancé she abandoned and journey across a magically-unpredictable continent. Can she keep the life she's given up everything to build?

Breaking Up the Royals: a king caught between love and legality...can Abbie and Edward's relationship survive engagement and the opposition who wants to tear them apart again?

Serving Side by Side: a security professional finds herself paired with a shy, sensory-sensitive man on the night watch. Can their friendship blossom into something more?

Bringing Down the King: a single mother gets her dream job as a journalist, only to find herself caught in royal scandal, opposing her son's new mentor. When forced to choose between love and her career, can she still come out a winner?

Winning Back the Duke: a doctor takes an expedition with her brother's best friend that has life-changing results. Can she resist the underlying attraction that's been there for years?

Acknowledgments

TO MY EDITORIAL TEAM at Salt and Sage: you all rock. I can't say it enough: your professionalism, straight-up knowledge of your genres, and kindness make this so much easier. Mehr, thank you for your expertise.

To my critique partners, Angela Boord, Ruth Hersey, and Kristin Houlihan: you are all so good at picking out the little discontinuities, the little moments that could be amped up, pulling out what's good, but could be better. I'm so blessed that you enjoy reading my work.

To Meghan Lloyd: thank you for your wonderful beta services! I appreciate you.

To my proofreader, Liz Schandorff: I keep waiting for you to tell me you're tired of doing this. Are you sure I can't pay you?

To my cover artist, Seth Smith: You're a joy! I'm going to miss working together, but I hope our paths continue to cross. At least I can say I knew you before you were famous.

And last, but certainly not least, thank you to my CFO, Mr. West. You're the marshmallows in my dairy-free cocoa, sweetheart. Keep being yourself, because that's who I love.

Connect with Fiona!

Thanks so much for taking the time to sample my work. I hope you enjoyed reading it even more than I enjoyed writing it, though I doubt that's possible. Being an author is a dream come true, and getting to share my books with delightful, thoughtful readers like you just adds to the sweetness. Drop me a line and let me know what you thought or leave a review on Goodreads!

Sign up for my bi-monthly newsletter, The West Wind, for freebies, deleted scenes, book reviews, and insight into my writing process at https://www.subscribepage.com/timber-falls.

On Twitter as @FionaWestAuthor[1]
On Facebook as @authorfionawest[2]
On Instagram as fionawestauthor[3]
On Goodreads as Fiona West[4]
Or email me at fiona@fionawest.net.
I love talking to fans!

---

1. https://twitter.com/FionaWestAuthor

2. https://web.facebook.com/authorfionawest/

3. https://www.instagram.com/fionawestauthor/

4. https://www.goodreads.com/author/show/18433825.Fiona_West